Pink Slippers, Bat Mitzvah Blues

Pink Slippers, Bat Mitzvah Blues

BY FERIDA WOLFF

The Jewish Publication Society
Philadelphia - Jerusalem

Manufactured in the United States of America.

Library of Congress Cataloging-in-Publication Data

Wolff, Ferida, 1946–
Pink slippers, bat mitzvah blues / Ferida Wolff. — 1st ed.
    p.   cm.
Summary: Thirteen-year-old Alyssa tries to balance the conflicting
demands of ballet training with finding her place as a Jew in
today's world.
    Cloth, ISBN 0–8276–0332–0
    Paperback, ISBN 0–8276–0531–5
    [1. Jews—United States—Fiction.   2. Ballet dancing—Fiction.
3. Dancers—Fiction.]   I. Title.
PZ7.W818554Pi   1989   89-1840
[Fic]—dc19   CIP
                                                                    AC

With love for Stephanie,
my daughter and technical advisor

In memory of Rabbi Edwin N. Soslow
for the kind of person he was

CHAPTER 1

I closed my Hebrew book with a sharp slap. It was the end of the last Hebrew class before my bat mitzvah. It was also the end of five years of Hebrew school, eight years of Sunday school, and six months of bat mitzvah training. After Saturday, my days would be my own, to spend doing the only thing in the world that mattered to me—dancing.

I gathered my things and raced for the door. With

a quick backward wave, I called out "Good-bye, Mrs. Hershkowitz" and nearly bumped into Rabbi Pearlman, who was standing just outside.

"I'm glad I caught you, Alyssa," Rabbi Pearlman said. "I'd like to speak with you for a moment."

I knew what was coming. He was going to give me the "It's a mitzvah to continue your Jewish education" speech. My older brother, Brad, had told me about it when he had his bar mitzvah three years ago.

"He gives it to all the kids," Brad said. "He wants you to come back for confirmation class. And he doesn't give up easily."

Brad, who is good at cartooning, made a poster with Rabbi Pearlman staring straight ahead and pointing his finger like the man in recruitment posters. Instead of Uncle Sam's top hat, he showed the rabbi with a blue and white striped yarmulke. Underneath he lettered the words: RABBI PEARLMAN WANTS YOU. I thought Brad would get into trouble when he showed it to the rabbi, but Rabbi Pearlman clapped his hands and cried "That's perfect!" and hung it on the bulletin board outside his office. Brad was confirmed last spring.

"Come," the rabbi said. "Let's go to my study

where it's a little quieter." He laughed. "I mean, where it's a lot quieter."

We walked through the crowded hallway, past Brad's poster, and into the rabbi's study.

"Well, now, Alyssa," said Rabbi Pearlman, "Saturday is the big day."

I nodded.

"I know you'll do a beautiful job up on the *bimah*. You read well, your chanting is fine, and you know the prayers. It will be a pleasure for me to share this simcha with you."

"Thank you, Rabbi," I said, waiting.

"But you know that just because you become a bat mitzvah, you don't suddenly stop being Jewish. There are certain responsibilities that go along with being a daughter of the commandment."

Here it comes, I thought.

"For years you have studied Hebrew so you could read the prayers. You learned about our holidays and the history of our people. While it must have seemed like a lot to you, it was only in preparation for understanding what it all means; *that* you get in confirmation class. You can finish the year out in your regular Hebrew class or you can join us right now. Our discussions go on all year. We are currently discussing the status of the Arabs in the state of Israel—"

"I'm not going to confirmation class," I interrupted. I wanted to stop Rabbi Pearlman before he really got wound up with the subject as he did with his sermons. It would make it harder for me to say no.

"But, Alyssa, you're such a good student. You know it's a mitzvah to continue your Jewish education," Rabbi Pearlman said.

"Yes," I whispered, trying not to laugh.

"It would be a shame to go through the mechanical work and not allow yourself to enjoy the interesting part. Next year we will be studying the Jewish theater. Mrs. Hershkowitz mentioned you are interested in the performing arts, am I right?"

"Ballet," I said.

"Well, this would be right up your alley."

I was about to tell Rabbi Pearlman that ballet was very different from the Jewish theater, but he went right on with his speech.

"And we will be going on special trips to other congregations to observe their services, so that you will feel at home in any synagogue you enter."

"I'm sorry, Rabbi—"

"And wait until Purim! The confirmation class is

going to put on a Purimspiel for the whole Hebrew school."

"Rabbi, I can't—"

"Don't say can't. We can do anything, with God's help," Rabbi Pearlman said. "Maybe you just need a little time off from your studies. I'll put your name down on the list for next year."

I shook my head. Brad had warned me it would be hard to say no to Rabbi Pearlman, but I had to, I must, if I wanted to become a dancer. There was just not enough time for both.

"I don't understand why you don't want to go to confirmation class," my mother said for the thousandth time since I had broken the news to her. She ladled out soup into the bowl I was holding.

"I wanted to make this for Friday night, but I thought with your grandparents coming over for dinner, perhaps we should be a little more traditional. I'll make chicken soup and challah."

"Grandma once told me chicken soup is boring," I said. "She said she put in cayenne pepper to give it a little 'zip.'"

"So that's why I was always so thirsty on Friday nights," Mom said. "Well, she is going to have to be bored this time."

I laughed to think of my grandmother sabotaging the Sabbath soup. I put out the soup bowls.

"Will you please call everyone to dinner, Lyssa?" my mother said.

"Dinner!" I yelled from where I was standing.

"Honestly, Lyssa, I could have done that myself."

Brad came charging up from the basement.

"Wash your hands, Brad," said my mother as he headed for the table. "Have you been finger painting down there?"

"No," said Brad. "It's only marker." He held up his stained hands. "I was coloring in my latest cartoon adventure of Mystery Man. You see, Mystery Man is about to walk across a rope strung between two ninety-story buildings, only he doesn't know that his old enemy, Grimes, has tampered with the rope. . . ."

My mother pointed to the sink.

"It won't come off anyway," he grumbled on his way to wash.

My father ambled into the kitchen in his blue sweatshirt. I knew exactly where he had been. He develops his own photographs and always wears that same sweatshirt. It's like a uniform.

"Working in the darkroom, Dad?" I asked.

"Uh, huh. I'm getting the cameras ready for Saturday night.

"Are you sure your father doesn't mind taking pictures at the reception, David?" Mom asked.

"You mean the king of the candid shot? He loves taking unposed photographs."

"But, Daddy," I cried. "Grandpa always takes close-ups of noses."

"Yeah," chimed in Brad. "I have pictures of noses I don't even recognize in my bar mitzvah album."

"Don't worry, Alyssa. I bought extra film so we can throw away Grandpa's noses and still have plenty of pictures left. Is that hot and sour soup I smell?"

"I *did* call everyone to dinner," my mother said, "or rather Lyssa did."

"Well, what are we waiting for?" my father said, heading for the table. He is a great one for eating dinner on time, on time being whenever *he* is ready.

"Lyssa doesn't want to go on with confirmation studies, David," Mom said as we sat down to eat.

"Have you thought about it, Alyssa?" my father asked. "Brad seemed to enjoy the class . . ."

"That was Brad," I said. "He also likes to draw cartoons. I don't."

"But, Lyssa, 'it's a mitzvah to continue your Jewish education,'" said Brad.

I glared at him. Brad laughed and slurped his soup.

"Don't slurp, Brad," said Mom.

Brad stopped slurping. Instead, he nearly choked. "What is this stuff?" he asked. "I thought it was Chinese hot and sour soup."

"Did *I* say it was Chinese hot and sour soup?" Mom retorted. "I just said it was hot and sour soup, that's all."

"Well, what kind of hot and sour soup is this, Rhoda?" asked Dad, cautiously lifting his spoon to his lips.

"It's Hot and Sour Sole Soup," Mom said.

"You mean it's got pigs' feet in it?" Brad asked, horrified.

"It isn't soul soup, it's *sole* soup. Sole, as in fish."

"You know I hate fish, Mom. Ever since you became a recipe-tester for *Wonderful Foods* Magazine, we have been eating some pretty strange stuff."

"Sole soup isn't that strange, and you can't even taste the fish because of the spices."

"I can and I'm not eating it."

"I have thought about it," I said, picking up the conversation from before. "I've thought about it every Monday and Wednesday for the past two years. I've thought about it each time my ballet class learned a new variation and I was a day behind, struggling to catch up. I've thought about it whenever I had to miss a rehearsal because I had Hebrew or Sunday school."

"We'd like you to give it a try, at least," Mom said.

"What's the point?" I asked. "I'd just quit in the middle."

"How do you know? Maybe you'll like it. It's not as if you'll be going by yourself. Most of your friends will be in your class."

"You always tell me to think for myself and now you want me to do something because everyone else is doing it."

"It's just that, well, I never had the opportunity to go to Hebrew school or to be confirmed and now I think I missed out on something."

"Then, *you* go to confirmation class," I said.

"Watch it," said my father. "Only the soup is supposed to be hot and sour tonight."

"That's it," Mom said. "If you don't like it, don't eat it. I'll just tell my editor that Mrs. Woonsprocket's recipe did not pass the taste test."

Mom cleared the soup bowls from the table and

returned with a casserole that was divided into three colors. We all stared at it. For a painting, it wasn't bad. For dinner, it was definitely questionable. Mom saw our questioning faces. She sighed.

"This is called Life, Liberty, and the Pursuit of Eggplant Casserole."

"Is this another of Mrs. Woonsprocket's creations, Mom?" I asked as she dished it onto my plate.

"No. Mrs. Harbinger-Smith of Philadelphia sent it in."

"Aw, Mom, can't we have a normal meal once in a while?" moaned Brad.

"You had lamb chops yesterday and chicken the day before."

"You mean Tía Maria's Chicken Olé?" said Brad. "It had string beans and chili peppers in it!"

"String beans are good for you," Mom said. "Although I'm not so sure about those peppers."

"But, Mom . . ."

"Think of it as broadening your culinary horizons," said Mom.

She finished serving the casserole. It sat on our plates, staring back at us. I poked it with my fork. It didn't look promising.

"Can we get back to what we were discussing?"

I said. "It isn't as if I plan to use the time to hang out on street corners and get into trouble. I need it to improve my technique."

"I think she's just tired from studying for her bat mitzvah, Rhoda," said Dad. "Let's leave her alone until after Saturday."

"It won't make any difference," I said. "I don't see why I should have to be confirmed if I don't want to be."

"I just don't want you to lose your Jewishness," my mother said.

"I don't have to sit in a classroom to feel Jewish, Mom. That's inside me. But I do have to be in dance class if I am going to get anywhere. The other girls take class six days a week—seven during performances."

"It doesn't seem natural . . ." Mom began.

I tried to keep calm, but my voice trembled. Couldn't they see that a ballet dancer didn't get very far if she didn't dance? No matter how hard I worked, I could see the other kids in class improving their technique faster than I was just because they were in class more often.

"Surely a day or two out of class couldn't make that much difference," said Dad.

"If you miss one day, you know it. If you miss two days, your class knows it. If you miss three days, *everybody* knows it."

"Who told you that?"

"My dance teacher, Nadine Perrin. She used to dance with the North Lakes Ballet. She said that whenever a dancer was absent, her teacher made her come in an hour early to warm up. Otherwise she would not be able to keep up with the class."

"I don't know, Alyssa," Mom said. "We've let you take dance because it seemed so important to you, but we don't like the idea of you being so obsessed with it."

"I'm just trying to broaden my cultural horizons," I replied.

Brad snickered.

"And what will happen to the rest of you if all you do is dance?"

"There won't *be* any rest of me if I don't dance," I said. "That is what I am—a dancer."

My parents looked questioningly at each other across the table.

"You're right, Mom, you don't understand!" I cried, and ran from the table. Life, Liberty, and the Pursuit of Eggplant was left uneaten on my plate.

CHAPTER 2

I recited my haftorah portion for my best friend, Ellen Ruben, in my bedroom after school on Thursday.

"Well?" I asked.

"It was perfect," said Ellen. "You didn't mess up once. I hope I do as well when I have my bat mitzvah."

"Don't worry," I said. "Mrs. Hershkowitz works

with you. You'll be ready. Besides, you can sing, so your chanting will sound good. I didn't even make the chorus at school. I know how to work my legs, but my voice has a life of its own."

"You sound wonderful," said Ellen. She hugged me. "I'm so excited. It's on Saturday. Do you believe it?"

"It's about time," I said. "The sooner it happens, the sooner I can quit."

I might have quit long ago except that my parents kept urging me to try it for another month or two, or until midyear, or just until after the holidays, which meant any time from Rosh Hashanah and Yom Kippur in the fall to Hanukkah in winter to Passover in the spring. By then, it made sense to finish out the year.

"What gets me," I said, "is why my parents even care. My mother told me she never even went to Hebrew school at all."

"That's funny," said Ellen. "My mother didn't either, yet she's the one who is pushing this bat mitzvah. She's starting on me now for confirmation class."

"Wait until Rabbi Pearlman gets started on you."

"RABBI PEARLMAN WANTS *YOU*," said Ellen.

"He does, too," I said. "I almost had to shout to make him listen to me when I told him I wasn't going to study for confirmation. He just didn't want to hear it."

I put away my books and took a burgundy leotard from my dresser drawer.

"Time for dancing already?" asked Ellen.

"It's always time for dancing," I said.

In fact, there had never been a time when I hadn't danced, except when I was a baby. I have pictures in my scrapbook of me in a pink tutu at age three. I went to Miss Marie's Dance Academy then. Mom said I was the only one in the recital who knew the steps. The picture shows everyone going in different directions, though, so you can't really tell who's doing the right steps and who's all wrong. I can't remember any of it, and if I didn't have that picture, I would have thought my mother had made up the whole story.

I fished around for a clean pair of pink tights and cried out triumphantly as I discovered a practically unused pair in the pile of dingy gray ones.

"It's an omen," I said as I dangled the floppy pink legs in front of Ellen. "Clean tights mean a clean start."

Ellen sneezed.

"See, it's true. My grandmother always says if someone sneezes after you say something, then that thing must be true."

"The only thing that's true is that I have a cold," said Ellen. She sneezed again.

"Well, get over it fast. You can't be sick on Saturday. I need my best friend near me or I'll never get through the service."

"Oh, I'll be there," Ellen said. "I just don't know in what condition. My nose is already red."

"It looks good with your hazel eyes," I said.

Ellen threw a pillow at me.

When Ellen left, I went to the bathroom and stuck my head under the sink faucet. I let the water trickle over my long, thick brown hair until it was wet enough to stay in place. Then I brushed it straight back and scooped it up with my hand, twisting the wet strands around and around until a tight knot was formed. I pinned the hair down into a bun, the only acceptable hairdo in Nadine's class. Then I jumped a few times on the blue bathroom tile to see if it would shake loose. A hairpin popped out. I pressed it back in and added another. If only I had Ellen's hair. It is the same color as mine but fine and silky. My hair is so thick, that I am always popping hairpins. There is nothing more annoying than having my hair come out in the middle of a combination. It is unprofessional, Nadine says, and I certainly do not want to be unprofessional. I wrapped a hair net around the straining bun.

"Now, stay there," I told it.

I checked the flowered dancing bag to make sure everything I needed for class was in it: pink ballet slippers, leg warmers, T-shirt, new pink satin pointe shoes, old dingy gray ones, extra hairpins, towel. I wear the leg warmers and T-shirt to warm up my muscles before class but once Nadine arrives, they have to come off. She doesn't want anything to "break the line" of the dancer's body. I use the old pointe shoes for familiar work and save the new ones for partnering where I need the extra support. Actually, I like stiff shoes during partnering just in case my partner loses his grip and lets go of me. A fifteen-year-old boy does not exactly inspire confidence when you are the tenth girl he is lifting and he looks tired. I would rather land on the hard box of the pointe shoe than on my poor toes. I already have a bunion. A dancer's body may be beautiful, but a dancer's feet are the ugliest things in the world.

The bag also contains my makeup case with pancake powder, lipstick, eye shadow, blush, eyeliner, and the long false eyelashes that highlight my eyes during performances. Nadine says a dancer is nothing without eyes, and all her dancers have dark, outlined eyes on stage. I once put on my stage makeup at home to see what it looked like in normal light. Dad was just walking in from work and stopped dead in his tracks.

"Don't you think your makeup is a little heavy, Lyssa?" he asked quietly. I could tell he was shocked and trying not to show it.

"Do you really think so, Daddy?" I said, fluttering my inch-long eyelashes at him. "Then, I'll go and take it off."

My father sighed in relief. It was nice to be able to do what my parents wanted once in a while without having to fight about it.

I grabbed the bag and went to say good-bye to Mom. I found her in the kitchen, punching dough.

"What's wrong, Mom?" I asked.

My mother always makes bread when she's upset. She says punching dough is more therapeutic and more socially acceptable than punching people.

"Oh, it's Uncle Stuart." Punch. "He just called to say he broke his leg last weekend and won't be able to read Saturday at services." Punch. "I'm going to ask Aunt Julia, but she hasn't come home from work yet, and who knows whether she'll want to do it on such short notice. I wish Uncle Stuart had called earlier." Punch. Punch. Punch.

"It's no big deal, Mom. He doesn't have to read."

"I know, but we had worked it all out, and now the timing of the service will be off, and I hate last-minute changes. Oh, dear, I've made too much dough. We'll be eating challah for the whole week."

"Freeze it," I said. I hoped she had made too much, because I love French toast made from the sweet, twisted bread. My mouth waters just thinking about it. Boy, could I get fat if I didn't have to watch my weight for dancing. All on challah French toast.

"I've got to go." I kissed my mother in mid-punch and went for my bike.

I really enjoy the bike ride to the studio. It gives me a chance to stop thinking about school and get my legs moving for dancing. As I get close to the studio, my worries about tests or homework seem to disappear. Snatches of music pop into my brain. I always have the feeling I am going to have the best class ever. Sometimes it is good, but sometimes I can't walk onto the wooden dance floor without tripping over my own feet. But good class or bad the feeling is always there.

I pedaled faster. I had a sense of anticipation

knowing that in only a few days I would be a full-time student in the professional division. I thought I might tell Cara but decided to wait. I imagined myself entering the mirrored studio Monday. Everyone would turn and stare in surprise, their faces reflected in the mirrors so that I would be the center of attention.

I smiled at the thought.

"Watch out, world; Alyssa's on the move," I said as I whizzed down Morrisey Street. A hairpin flew out of my bun, but I just laughed.

CHAPTER 3

"Let's go, everybody," Mom called out early Saturday morning. "This is not the time to dawdle. We want to get there before the family starts showing up."

"Take it easy, Mom," I said. "We'll get there on time."

"I have to speak to Rabbi Pearlman as soon as

we arrive and let him know that Aunt Julia will be reading in Uncle Stuart's place."

"I'll be ready in a minute, Mom. I have to fix my hair. It's a mess."

"Oh, for crying out loud, Alyssa. You look absolutely lovely. Now, please try to hurry. It's getting late."

"My hair is *not* lovely. Look at these bangs. If I comb them up, they're wild. If I comb them down, they're in my eyes. I can't read if my hair is in my eyes."

I played around with my hair in front of the hall mirror. Mom was fidgeting at the door. I wished I had some bread dough I could give her, but I didn't, and my hair just wouldn't be rushed.

"No one will even notice if your hair isn't perfect, Alyssa."

Brad came out of the kitchen dripping cookie crumbs onto the floor.

"Brad!" Mom shouted. "We're having people back to the house. Clean that up."

Brad passed me on his way to the broom closet.

"What happened to your hair?" he said.

"My hair? What do you mean, my hair?"

"Well, the bangs look funny."

"Mom, he noticed!"

"Alyssa, comb your bangs and let's get out of here. Your father is waiting outside."

The synagogue was already filling up with familiar faces by the time we arrived. Mom immediately went in search of Rabbi Pearlman. Dad put on his party smile and stood by the doorway to greet everyone. Brad went off to check on his poster.

I hoped Ellen would show up pretty soon.

"Mazel tov!" shouted Aunt Carol as she barreled her way down the hall to reach me.

"I haven't done it yet, Aunt Carol," I said.

"Well, you'll be beautiful, I know it, and I'll give you another mazel tov afterward." She put her arm around my shoulder and squeezed hard, then disappeared into the sanctuary to find a good seat.

I spotted Ellen, or rather heard Ellen, as she entered. She coughed, a loud, raspy cough that carried down the hall. She had promised me she'd come, but her cold had come with her, and it had gotten worse. I waved. Ellen waved back and made her way over.

"I couldn't wait for you to show up," I said. "I need someone to help me face all these relatives."

Ellen laughed and coughed. It took her a minute or so to stop.

"Sorry," she said.

"You sound awful."

"I know," Ellen said. "The cough medicine I took before leaving the house should start to work soon."

"Maybe you should go to the doctor."

"For a cough? I only go to the doctor if I'm dying."

"Oh, oh," I said. "Here come Great-uncle Henry and Great-aunt Ruth. Stay close. I need moral support. He's a questioner and she's an answerer."

"What's that?"

"You'll find out."

"Well, well, if it isn't little Alyssa, not so little anymore. How are you?"

"She's fine, Henry. See those rosy cheeks? You don't get rosy cheeks from being sick."

"Glad to hear it. And how are you doing in school? Hebrew school, that is?"

"How do you think she's doing, Henry," said Aunt Ruth. "Would she be having a bat mitzvah if she weren't doing well?"

"And how are your mother and father? I haven't seen them for such a long time."

"Go ask them yourself, Henry. They're right over there."

"Did you invite any friends today, Alyssa?"

"Look in front of you, Henry. Alyssa has a

young lady standing right next to her, so I guess she must have invited her friends."

"Well, we'd better go say hello to your parents, Alyssa," Uncle Henry said. "It was nice talking to you again, wasn't it?"

"It certainly was," said Aunt Ruth.

They kissed me and left.

Ellen and I smothered our laughs.

"A questioner . . ."

". . . and an answerer," finished Ellen.

Grandma and Grandpa Rappaport came over next. They hardly look like grandparents at all to me. Grandma, in a charcoal-gray wool suit with a thin silver thread running through it and a ruffled cranberry blouse might have been going to a business convention. Grandpa always looks the same in his pinstripe navy suit, pale-blue shirt, and paisley tie, which he wears to every family celebration. Sometimes I wonder if Grandpa sleeps in his suit.

"Are you nervous, honey?" asked my grandmother.

"Not really, Grandma," I answered.

"You both look wonderful," said my grandmother. "No longer the little girls I used to take to the park."

Then she leaned over and whispered to me, "I

can't wait until the reception where we plan to
shower you with gifts. I'm glad you decided to have
it at home, Alyssa. It's so much more intimate."
Grandpa patted my cheek.
"Come on, Lil, let's go in. I want a seat on the
aisle so I can see everything."
"Your grandparents never seem to get old," Ellen
said through another muffled cough.
"They don't have time to get old. They're too
busy traveling to Israel or Alaska or somewhere."
"My grandparents don't go anywhere," said
Ellen. "They hardly ever leave the house. My
grandmother cooks and my grandfather reads."
"It must be nice to have a grandmother who
makes chicken soup and matzoh balls," I said.
"Doesn't your grandma?"
"Not anymore," I said. "My family is weird." I
smiled, remembering what Mom had said about
Grandma's soup. "And you haven't met my father's
parents yet. Three years ago my grandmother decided it was time to write a book, so she wrote a
romance novel."
"Was it published?" asked Ellen.
"Not only was it published, but she signed a contract to write three more. She writes under the name
of Nerissa Knight, and all the covers on her books
show a woman with a skinny-minny waist and low-

cut dress swooning into some disgustingly-hand-
some man's arms."

"Wow," said Ellen. "How come you never told
me about that?"

"How can I go around telling people that my
grandmother writes trashy novels for a living?"

"What about your grandfather?"

"Oh, he's retired—at least he was until Grandma
started writing books. Then he went back to work
so she would have some time to herself. He says he
plans to retire as soon as my grandmother finishes
out her contract. *She* says she found her calling and
may never stop writing, so my grandfather may
never stop working."

"It's amazing your parents seem so normal," said
Ellen.

"Normal? They're the weirdest of all. My mother
makes beautiful food no one in her right mind
would eat and punches bread when she's upset. You
call that normal? And don't get me started on my
dad."

Rabbi Pearlman came out of his study with my
mother by his side. They walked over to us.

"Hello, Ellen," said the rabbi.

"Hello, Rabbi Pearlman."

"Ready, Alyssa?" he said.

"I guess so," I answered.

"Good. It's almost time for services to start."

He swept us into the sanctuary with the long sleeves of his black robe. Ellen slipped into a seat next to Brad while I took my place on the *bimah* with Rabbi Pearlman and Cantor Weiss.

I watched as the sanctuary filled with my relatives and friends and congregation members. My stomach tightened. It felt the way it does when I am onstage and the curtain is about to go up. I looked for my parents. They were sitting stiffly in the front row with Brad and Ellen. Ellen gave me the thumbs-up sign. Brad saw what Ellen had done and he turned thumbs down. Grandma, who sat in the second row just behind Brad, bonked him on the head. Then she blew me a kiss. I smiled and relaxed a little.

Rabbi Pearlman began the service. When we finished the *shema*, the prayer proclaiming the oneness of God, he nodded at me and I started the *v'ahavtah*. I read the Hebrew and then the English.

"Thou shalt love the Lord, thy God, with all thy heart, with all thy soul, and with all thy might . . ."

My voice sounded thin and very young.

I heard myself say "Please join me in responsive reading" and was surprised when the congregation did. The faces faded as I read my Torah and haftorah portions, the nervousness lessening as each hurdle was passed. And then suddenly, there were my parents, blessing me and saying how proud they were at this very special day in all our lives.

Rabbi Pearlman cleared his throat and addressed the congregation.

"Alyssa Stein has been with us in this congregation for many years as a child," he began. "She learned to read Hebrew, which she demonstrated so ably here today. She qualified for the Hebrew Honor Society. She participated in our tutoring program. She learned everything we had to teach her—as a child. But now she is no longer a child in our synagogue; Alyssa has become a full, participating member of this congregation. And while these coming years will be very busy ones for her, we hope she will take the time to be with us as often as she can. I have already spoken with her about our confirmation class and what a mitzvah it is to continue with her Jewish studies. Whether she chooses to do so or not, she knows she is always welcome within these walls."

He turned toward me.

"Alyssa, don't think that when you walk off the *bimah* today we never want to see your face up here again. You, and our other b'nai mitzvah, are our hope. You are our future. With you, we share our dreams; through you, we continue our heritage. We have come through centuries of change and devastation and survived as a people. That's because Judaism has a lot to offer. We take from Judaism what we need and give what we can. And the nice thing about Judaism is that it's always there for us—it is here for you, Alyssa. Don't give up on it."

Rabbi Pearlman paused and smiled.

My throat tightened. The years of annoyance at having to go to Hebrew school vanished. Am I doing the right thing? I wondered. A heavy feeling of responsibility settled over me, the way it does on Yom Kippur when we pray that we have been worthy of being inscribed in the book of life for another year.

I had taken all these years and now they were looking to me to give something back. But what could I give? Wasn't being Jewish enough or did I have to prove it in some way as well?

"Alyssa," Rabbi Pearlman continued, "it is with great pride in your Jewish accomplishment that I present you with this gift from Temple Beth Israel's sisterhood. Use it in good health."

I took the package Rabbi Pearlman handed to me. It was heavy, and I knew it was a set of Sabbath candlesticks from the Judaica shop. I looked out toward my parents sitting in the first row. I expected to see tears in Mom's eyes, which I did, but was startled to see that my father was teary-eyed too. Brad was grinning. The cantor burst into "*Oseh Shalom.*" Everyone joined in and then it was all over.

"Mazel tov!"

There was Aunt Carol, waiting for me as I stepped from the *bimah.* I laughed and hugged her. My parents tried to be dignified, but their broad smiles gave them away. I hugged them and Brad too. We walked down the aisle together toward the social hall, where Rabbi Pearlman waited with the wine-filled kiddush cup. He said the blessing. Everyone took a sip of wine and some sweets. The only thing I wanted was the small pink-iced cake that had ALYSSA written across it in white letters.

My bat mitzvah had come and gone. All that was left was the party. I was surrounded by a sea of mazel tovs and laughter and kisses; the heavy feelings and doubt disappeared. I had done what was expected of me. What more could anyone ask? Now, finally, I was free to dance!

4 CHAPTER

I was warming up at the dance studio on Monday when Kim walked in.

"You're here early," she said. She stretched her leg onto the barre.

"I'm a little stiff after the weekend," I said.

I had actually come in early to surprise everyone. After all, it was a Monday, a day I was usually at Hebrew school. I wondered why Kim didn't say anything. Well, I wouldn't say anything either until someone noticed.

I held onto the barre and started my routine with grands pliés. Heels together in first position, I bent my knees and slowly lowered my body. Halfway down, my knees cracked. And my parents can't understand why I need to dance every day.

I watched Kim grab the heel of her pink slipper and extend her leg straight up to her ear in an elegant stretch. It reminded me that I had to work on my own extension, which was good but not great. I sank to the floor in a split and sat there as the studio began filling up. Without straining my neck, all I could see was a forest of pink legs.

Pieces of conversation floated down.

". . . and I was sure he was going to drop me. It's scary enough being held high over someone's head on the end of an arm without worrying whether or not last night's fight might mean a quick trip to the floor."

That was Fawn. She has the perfect name for a ballerina. Her legs are as thin as a baby deer's and her leaps as graceful. At seventeen, she is the oldest and most accomplished girl in the school. She's working on the part of the Sugar Plum Fairy for our annual production of *The Nutcracker*, the only girl's part Nadine has assigned so far. It will be Fawn's last performance for the school because she has been accepted into the North Lakes Ballet Company and will be leaving after Christmas. I can't even begin to be jealous because the part is really too hard for me right now, but there's always next year. I know I'll be much better by then. Sugar Plum wears the most beautiful lacy purple tutu. It is covered with sequins that catch the spotlight and send out tiny glittering rays all over the stage.

Jason is the handsome cavalier. He's seventeen too and reminds me of Baryshnikov. I wonder if Baryshnikov has as bad a temper as Jason. He calls it "artistic temperament" whenever it gets out of hand. He'd be just a jerk except that he dances so well.

It makes me cry when Fawn and Jason dance together—it is so beautiful. They just started going out together, and it is a stormy romance. It's funny to see them smile at each other so lovingly during rehearsal and then scream and yell as soon as their pas de deux is over.

"I know Nadine will pick me for the solo. She said how good my variation was—oops, sorry, Alyssa."

Amy Sue tripped over me and went on walking.

Amy Sue Benedict is always tripping over things and bumping into people outside the studio. Last week she bumped against Janna at the soda machine in the hall. Janna spilled Diet Pepsi onto the floor and before she had a chance to wipe it up, Amy Sue slipped on the wet spot and landed smack on her bottom. Anyone watching would have sworn Amy Sue was an awful dancer but something magical happens when she crosses through the doorway into the studio; her body works. Her arms and legs are coordinated. And she looks good. So good, in fact, she sometimes gets the parts I try out for. But even Amy Sue tripping over me did not make her notice I was there on a Hebrew school day.

I pushed myself out of the split. It was all I could do to keep from shouting "Look at me. It's Monday. I'm here!" Instead, I took my place at the barre as Nadine entered the studio. Nadine will notice, I thought. But the music began and we started working. Pliés, tendus, battements, port de bras, extend and hold.

I got lost in the barre work. It was hard to concentrate on muscles and disappointment at the same time.

"Pointe shoes, girls," Nadine announced midway through class.

I was wrapping the shiny pink ribbons tightly
around my ankle when Nadine came over to me.

"No Hebrew school today, Alyssa?" she asked.

"I've finished," I said, happy that Nadine had noticed after all. "I'll be coming to class every day
from now on."

"Good," said Nadine. "Now you can finally
work on your technique without being distracted by
outside activities."

Nadine clapped her hands, and the girls scurried
back to the barre.

My happiness faded. I had always considered Hebrew school "a distracting outside activity" but
hearing Nadine say it made me need to defend myself for going all of those years. I slipped in last and
took my place behind Kim.

"It wasn't just an outside activity," I muttered as
I struggled to balance in relevé. "It was important."

"What?" whispered Kim.

"Nothing," I whispered back.

"Other side, girls," called out Nadine.

I turned around and planted myself firmly in fifth
position. "It was," I repeated.

I called Ellen when I got home.

"No one noticed?" Ellen asked.

"Nadine did, but no one else said anything," I said.

"That's probably because they expect to see you. They don't think of the days."

"I guess you're right. It just seemed so special to me that it was a Monday, and I was there."

"Hold on," said Ellen suddenly.

I heard Ellen cough violently on the other end. It was the kind of cough that went on and on. When Ellen finally finished, she sounded exhausted.

"Did you go to the doctor?" I asked.

"Nope," Ellen said.

"You sound as if you're dying."

"No one ever died from a cough," she said. "Besides, if I'm sick, I don't want to know. It will go away eventually. They always tell you they can't do anything for a cold anyway."

"I don't know, El. That sounds like more than a cold to me."

"Well, then, what do you prescribe, Dr. Stein?"

"Get plenty of rest and drink lots of liquid. That's what my grandmother always tells me."

"Does your grandmother also tell you how to get plenty of rest when you have three tests tomorrow, a term paper due in two weeks, and a bat mitzvah hanging over your head in a few months? I'm panicking already."

"The only other piece of advice she gives me is to laugh a lot," I said.

"What?" said Ellen.

"She read this book that said the human body can heal itself by laughing."

"Then, tell me something funny so I can laugh."

The only funny thing I could think of at that moment was the hair coming out of Mr. Ryeback's ears. Mr. Ryeback is our history teacher. He likes to dramatize everything to make it "come alive" for us. He acted his little heart out to make the Mayflower Compact exciting, but all we can remember are the little squiggly brown hairs moving up and down as he talked. All I had to say was "Mayflower Compact" to Ellen and she got hysterical.

She laughed, all right, but it didn't make her better. In fact, she had such a bad coughing fit that . Mrs. Ruben took away the phone and told me Ellen had to get off.

CHAPTER 5

Ellen wasn't in school the next day.

Good, I thought. It's about time she used some sense. I went around to Ellen's teachers to get her homework and stopped at her house on the way home.

"Thank you, Alyssa," said Ellen's mother. "I'm afraid you can't see Ellen now. She's asleep."

"Will she be back in school tomorrow, Mrs. Ruben?"

"I don't think so. She has a little fever and her cough is pretty bad. If it doesn't clear up in a day or two, she'll have to see the doctor, like it or not."

"Please tell her I'll call later," I said.

"I will. And I know she'll appreciate getting the homework assignments. She gets so far behind when she misses a day."

"I know. They really pile it on. Every teacher thinks *his* subject is the only thing in the world that matters. Well, 'bye, Mrs. Ruben."

When I got home, I found my mother knuckle-deep in cottage cheese.

"What's that?" I asked nervously.

"I'm making something really interesting to-night," Mom said. "It's called Cheese It, the Crops. You start with a layer of onions, then add a layer of zucchini, a layer of carrots, some broccoli florets, cover the whole thing with a cottage cheese paprika sauce, and garnish with asparagus spears radiating from the center."

"Is that dinner, Mom?" I asked. "Can I just have a salad?"

"I need your expert opinion on this, Lyssa. Mrs. Merriweather of Portland, Maine, is counting on it."

"I'll taste it," I said. It actually didn't sound *that* horrible.

The phone rang.

"Will you get that, Lyssa?"

I picked up the receiver. It was Rabbi Pearlman. I immediately forgot about my mother's weird concoction.

"So, Alyssa, it's all over," he said.

"Yes, Rabbi."

"You did a fine job Saturday."

"Thank you."

"I just called to let you know that our confirmation class will be having an informal dinner with B'nai Tikvah's tomorrow night. Besides meeting other kids in the neighborhood, there will be an opportunity to ask both Rabbi Hochberg and me questions about Judaism or about anything at all, for that matter. Kind of a 'Dear Rebbe' session. We would love to see you there, Alyssa."

"I'm sorry, Rabbi Pearlman, but I have dancing."

"I know, but I thought maybe if you just missed *one* class it wouldn't cause such a problem."

"It's getting close to *Nutcracker* time . . ."

"Oh, I see. Well, if you change your mind, I just wanted you to know."

"Thank you, Rabbi. Good-bye."

"Good-bye, Alyssa."

I hung up. Brad warned me that Rabbi Pearlman didn't give up easily. I looked at my watch. It was four-thirty. Between stopping at Ellen's and talking to Rabbi Pearlman, I was running late. I grabbed a blueberry muffin to munch on while I got ready for dancing. I was going to work my feet off in the next couple of weeks so I could get a good part in *The Nutcracker*. Last year I was only dancing corps parts, and although the Waltz of the Flowers is probably my favorite group piece, I really wanted a solo.

I would love to get the part of Dew Drop Fairy. She comes out in the midst of the flowers, and the audience always gasps. No one has ever gasped at me. It would be nice.

I wondered if Rabbi Pearlman disapproved of my being in a Christmas ballet. Maybe I shouldn't have said anything about it. Now he would really think I was giving up on Judaism.

I checked my watch again. If I didn't hurry, I'd never make the five o'clock class. I got my bike, slung my dancing bag over my shoulder, and wheeled down to the studio.

This time I was not early. I barely had five minutes to stretch out before class started. My barre work was passable, but my center work was not.

"Alyssa, turnout!" scolded Nadine.

I adjusted my hip.

"Piqué, piqué, chaîné, chaîné, chaîné," Nadine chanted as we took off from the corner of the room. My turns sent me spinning off into Amy Sue, throwing her off balance.

"Sorry," I mumbled.

She muttered something under her breath, realigned her body, and continued on to the opposite corner.

"Spot, Alyssa!" Nadine called out.

I refocused my eyes on a splotch of blue paint in the corner and started up again.

"Whip that head around. Whip. Whip. Whip."

I caught a glimpse of Nadine shaking her head as I passed in front of her, and it threw my timing off even more. This was not the way to get a solo, I told myself angrily.

"Bad day?" whispered Cara when I reached the other side.

I nodded. It was turning out to be a bad week. Yesterday nobody noticed me, and today I brought attention to myself by doing everything wrong. I was tempted to call Rabbi Pearlman and tell him I was coming. It would be a lot easier on my nerves. But that wouldn't make me the dancer I hoped to become. I took a deep breath and repeated the turns on my left side.

"Better, Alyssa," Nadine said as I passed her again. I concentrated on spotting so that I wouldn't get dizzy and lose my balance. When the last girl finished her turns, Nadine said, "We'll have three groups of six. Watch now."

Nadine stood in front and demonstrated a new combination for us by slowly marking the steps. We followed in back, walking through the glissades, the sliding steps; jetés, the jumps; and pas de chat, the cat steps. We motioned the pirouettes, the tight whirls on one leg, with our hands. It was a shorthand that saved energy until it was really needed.

"All set, girls?" Nadine asked after we had run through the combination twice. "The first group, please."

Amy Sue rushed to the front. Fawn and Janna followed. Cara waved to me, and with Jennifer we made up the second row. I try to get into the first group so I can do it again if I have to. Today seemed like a "have to" day.

"One note before you start," said Nadine. "You

may do more than one pirouette; but they must be done right. Better one perfect pirouette than three or four or even five sloppy ones. Ready? And . . ."

We glided into the combination.

I had been practicing pirouettes in the kitchen and had finally been able to do three full turns. But what I thought were perfect turns in the kitchen suddenly seemed less than wonderful under Nadine's demanding eye. I did one careful pirouette. We finished in fifth position, changed direction, and repeated the exercise.

"Not bad for a first time, girls," said Nadine. "Second group, please."

For Nadine to say that, we must have done it perfectly. Cara nudged me with her elbow as we made way for the next group. I decided not to go with the next group. I didn't want to push my luck.

After the third group completed the combination, we did it all again. Nadine's voice floated over the music, singing out the French words. She once told us that all ballet instructions are given in French. Even when a dancer doesn't how how to speak Russian or Yugoslavian or any language other than her own, she can take ballet class anywhere in the world because the words will be the same.

"Now we will do grands jetés en tournant from

the corner. Don't let the leg drop after the turn,
girls. When you complete a movement, do not stop;
continue until you run out of floor, and pay particular attention to your arms. Don't flap your wings
for balance. We want ballet dancers, not ducks migrating. Ready? Fawn, you begin.''

Fawn readied herself and the music started. I
watched her arms. They swept gracefully over her
head as she leaped up and turned in midair. She
landed softly and, without losing a beat, went into
the next one. Fawn was no migrating duck. Amy
Sue, who came after her, was. She had trouble bal-
ancing as she came out of the jump and used her
arms to keep herself from falling. When she finished
at the other end of the studio, she stamped her foot
in frustration. It was comforting to see that Amy
Sue could mess up just as much as I could. When
it was my turn, I concentrated on not flapping my
wings. I was better than Amy Sue but not as good
as Fawn.

"Look," Nadine said before she had us change to
the other side. "Look at how it should be."

Nadine walked deliberately to one end of the studio and planted herself firmly in position. Then she
took off, literally, into the air. She went up and out.
Her arms had a life of their own as they effortlessly

glided to their proper places. Her turns were sharp and clean. Eighteen pairs of eyes followed her movements, and when she stopped, we burst into applause. Nadine didn't demonstrate full out very often, but when she did, there was no doubt as to why she had once been the principal ballerina of the North Lakes Ballet.

"Ooooh," breathed out Cara.

I was still holding my breath. I was going to be like that. One day, I would dance like Nadine.

6 CHAPTER

Ellen sounded worse when I called on Wednesday.

"A-huh, a-huh," she coughed feebly. "Oooh, that hurt."

"When are you going to the doctor, Ellen?" I asked. I had been trying to get her to go for days, but she insisted the cough wasn't that bad. Now she couldn't pretend anymore; every time she started to talk, she began to cough, and then she had to take a minute or two to catch her breath.

"My mother, a-huh, is about, a-huh, to take me, a-huh." She went off into a coughing spasm that left her moaning.

"I'll call you tomorrow, okay?" I told Ellen.

There was no answer.

"Ellen? Are you there?" I shouted into the phone.

"Don't yell. I'm sick, not deaf," she said.

"But you didn't answer."

"I nodded my head."

"I didn't hear it rattle. Take it easy."

I wasn't really too worried about Ellen. She is stubborn. She wouldn't let a little thing like a bad cough keep her out of action. I remember when she had the flu last year. She didn't let it stop her. She said it had three days of her valuable time and no more. On the fourth day, Ellen was back in school, cracking jokes at lunchtime and being her usual energetic self. A week later she smashed in the winning goal that won the championship for her soccer team.

Even so, I stared at the phone for a while until my stomach started rumbling. I went in search of my pre-dancing snack. I wouldn't be eating dinner until eight o'clock, and I needed sustenance.

I found my mother in the kitchen. Today, she was testing Veal Good Turnovers.

I opened the refrigerator and pulled out ingredients for a salad. I would rather have been making a hot fudge sundae with chocolate-chocolate-chip ice cream. But a dancer's body does not make allowances for hot fudge sundaes. It would take a week to work it off. Only sometimes, for very special occasions, is it worth the bother. When Ellen got better, I would make us two huge sundaes just dripping with fudge.

I watched Mom make the turnovers while I ate my salad. She cut five-inch circles from pastry dough she had rolled out. Onto each circle, she placed a mixture of ground veal, onions, parsley, bread crumbs, and spices. Then she folded half the circle over the filling to meet the other edge of the circle. She dipped her finger into a small dish of water and wet the bottom rim of the dough. With a fork, she pressed the two edges together to seal them in, making a striped design. With leftover dough, she made tiny leaves, which she attached to the turnover. Finally, she brushed egg over the whole thing. The egg would help the dough to brown. Not everything Mom makes tastes wonderful, but the food always looks pretty.

"Ellen's finally going to the doctor," I said.

"That bad cold of hers," said Mom.

"Yes." I fiddled with a slice of cucumber. "Do you think it's more serious than a cold, Mom?"

"It's always best to wait for the results of an examination before making a diagnosis," Mom said.

Mom used to be a nurse before she had kids and started testing recipes. She set the oven temperature for 350 degrees.

I hung around while Mom put the turnovers onto a baking sheet and into the oven. I followed her from the oven to the counter, to the pantry and back to the counter.

"For goodness' sake, Lyssa, I can't move around here without bumping into you," said Mom.

"Sorry."

I moved out of her way but still did not leave the kitchen. Mom looked at me, ready to scold, but then her face softened. She came over and put her arm around me.

"I'm sure Ellen will be all right," she said.

"I know," I said. "I'm not worried." I hugged my mother. Well, maybe I was a *little* worried. Just then Brad buzzed in, his radio earphones attached to his head.

"What's new?" he said.

"Ellen went to the doctor," I told him.

"Why? She break a leg or something?"

"She has a cold."

"How boring," said Brad. Then his eyes lit up. "Maybe it isn't a cold at all. Maybe she has a rare disease and will have to be sent away to the desert for 'the cure.'"

"Mom," I shouted, "is he right?"

"Since when is Brad a doctor?" Mom said, annoyed. "Why do you have to tease your sister all the time, young man?"

"It isn't *all* the time," Brad said. "Anyway, doesn't that sound like a good episode for Mystery Man? Mystery Man comes down with some rare tropical disease that can only be cured by drinking the special waters from one particular oasis in the Sahara Desert. While he's traveling by camel to get to the oasis, he overhears the camel driver plotting with his men to seal off the water and charge enormous fees for its use. Naturally, Mystery Man, being the champion of the needy and being in need himself of the water, will find a way to foil their dastardly plan. . . ."

I sneaked out of the kitchen as Brad cornered Mom at the sink.

At dancing, I stood at the end of the barre so I could look in the skinny mirror. Some of the mirrors make me look fat, others make me look skinny. Just thinking about the ice cream sundae I was going to make for Ellen and me when she got well made me suck in my stomach. I nodded to my skinny image across the room. It nodded back. While I was staring, I evaluated my legs. They were long and thin with just a bit too much knee. I would give anything to look like Fawn. I automatically looked to the place where Fawn always stands. I was surprised to see she wasn't in class.

Fawn came in just as the music began and slipped in behind me. I could hear her breathing hard as though she had been running. Even Fawn, Nadine's absolute favorite, wouldn't dare be late for class. I moved up a little and brushed against Amy Sue. Amy Sue shuffled forward and bumped into Cara, who knocked into Kim. It was dominoes all along the barre.

"My, we have a big class," said Nadine. "I'm glad to see that everyone is here, but it does crowd up the barre a bit. We need a lot of room, especially today, for our exercises. We are going to work on our legs and we will need a full swing for the battements en cloches, so spread out."

Everyone shifted position. I tried an experimental developpé devant, a front leg extension, and found

my toes in Amy Sue's back, but if I moved backward,
I would be up against Fawn. It was the same for everyone.

Uh, oh, I thought. I knew what it meant—the center barre. Sure enough, Nadine opened the storage
closet where the portable barre is kept when not in
use. I lowered my eyes so she would not notice me.
I hate that barre. I never feel secure when we lean over
even though Nadine pairs us off two on each side to
balance it. And the worst part is that the center people
have to look in the fat mirror.

"The last four girls on the end come to the center,
please," said Nadine.

It figured. I trudged to the middle of the floor but
refused to look in the mirror until I absolutely had to.

"All right, now," Nadine began, "let us really
work today. We need to build stamina. I will start
selecting dancers for *The Nutcracker* next week. There
will be a sheet tacked to the bulletin board with role
assignments."

An excited murmur rose throughout the room.

"If your name does not appear the first day, don't
panic. I will be adding names as the week progresses.
Some of you may get the same parts you had last year;
some may get entirely new parts. Some of you may
have solo parts; others may not. Everyone, except for

the Dew Drop and Sugar Plum fairies, will be in the corps at one time or another."

I couldn't help crossing my fingers. I wanted a solo more than anything in the world.

"But *this* is the time to work, not when you are about to go on stage. Don't think that weeks of goofing off won't show in the glare of the lights; sloppy work screams out to the audience. Those people out there pay good money to see us perform, and they want their money's worth. This is a professional production, not a recital. So if you goof off, you get out. If you miss three rehearsals, you're also out."

Amy Sue raised her hand.

"Yes, Amy Sue?" Nadine said.

"What if you get sick or something?"

"Three strikes and you're out. It would have to be an excuse that would melt a statue's heart for me to break the rule." Nadine looked around. "Is that clear?"

We nodded. Nadine always gives us a speech before we go into rehearsal for a ballet. It is sort of a pep talk in reverse; instead of getting us up and screaming, it quiets us down and makes us worry.

"Oh, one more thing," said Nadine. "If you think you won't have to relearn a part you did last year, think again. Your body may remember the steps, but

I can teach those to anybody off the street. It is only constant practice that gives the dance the precision and beauty that turns foot shuffling into art. So let's practice."

With straight backs and rounded arms, and only an occasional creak of a knee, we began our pliés.

CHAPTER  7

I saw Ellen the next day for only a short while but long enough to find out that Brad was partially right—it wasn't just a cold. Ellen had pneumonia. When I heard that, I got really scared. I thought people died from pneumonia, but I didn't tell Ellen that. I just asked how she felt.

"Rotten," she said. "And I know I look a mess. I can't even brush my hair. Whenever I move, and sometimes when I don't, I cough, and it hurts like anything."

She pointed to her night table. Beside the familiar tulip petal lamp and clock radio were a pitcher of water, a small drinking glass, and bottles of medicine.

"Do you know what they gave me?" she said. "Expectorant—to make me cough more! They don't care how much it hurts."

Ellen had been attempting little spurts of coughs, and she was talking as if she were holding back. Now the cough burst through and she gasped. I held my breath until she had finished.

"Are you all right?" I asked.

"No," she said. "But thanks for asking."

She sank back in bed, barely breathing. I tried to get her to laugh or talk or play a game but she wasn't interested in anything. All she did was cough and each time Ellen coughed, she shuddered. All her energy seemed to have left her.

When I went back home, I caught Mom in the kitchen gathering her utensils for baking. Before she got involved, I asked her about Ellen. She said Ellen would get better if she took her medication and rested in bed. That scared me even more.

"She won't do it, Mom," I said. "Ellen hates taking medicine and she won't stay in bed. She doesn't even sleep late on weekends."

"She won't have much of a choice," said Mom. "The medicine will make her drowsy, and she really won't feel up to doing anything, so she'll stay in bed."

I thought about that for a minute. It didn't seem like Ellen would be interested in getting up and around quite yet, but you never could tell. I hoped she would have enough sense to do what she was supposed to.

"Maybe you're right, Mom. Ellen said it hurt to move. She sounded as if she were in agony when she coughed."

"Then, she must have pleurisy as well," Mom said.

"Pleurisy? Is that anything like leprosy?" I asked fearfully.

Mom laughed. "No. There's a membrane lining the inside of the chest and the lungs called the pleura. When that gets irritated, it's called pleurisy. That's what's causing Ellen the pain. The medicine she's taking will help ease that."

Brad emerged from his cartoon cave in the basement and plunked his latest masterpiece down on the kitchen table.

"You'll have to move that," said Mom. "I need the table to roll out the dough for the strudel. It has to be done the old-fashioned way—stretched out and rolled paper-thin."

Brad picked up his paper. "I'm afraid to ask what's going in it," he said.

"Nothing exotic," Mom said. "This is Grandma's recipe. It has raisins and nuts, cinnamon and cloves, and layers of flaky pastry."

"Who's coming?" he asked suspiciously.

Brad and I had learned that Mom only tries out her weird recipes on us. She makes normal food for everyone else.

"No one. I just thought we needed a break from 'cute food' for a while."

I kissed her.

"Thanks, Mom. I love Grandma's strudel. May I bring some get-well strudel to Ellen?"

"Of course, but she won't have much of an appetite right now."

"Then, I'll freeze a piece and bring it to her another time."

"By the way, Lyssa," Brad said, "Rabbi Pearlman called while you were out."

"Again?" I said.

"Remember . . ." said Brad.

"He doesn't give up easily!" we said together.

I laughed. "Did he say what he wanted?"

"Yes. He asked if you could come in two weeks and help decorate the sukkah for Sukkot services on Sunday night."

"Why me?"

"Because decorating the sukkah is the job of the confirmation class," Brad said.

"But I'm not even in the confirmation program," I complained. "I told him that."

"*You* may have said no, but it hasn't registered with Rabbi Pearlman yet."

Actually, I wouldn't mind doing it. There is something special about Sukkot, a happy holiday after the more serious holidays of Rosh Hashanah and Yom Kippur. The sukkah was built each year in the inner courtyard. The middle grades of the Hebrew school gathered leaves and branches for the open roof; the younger grades made fall decorations, and the confirmation class put it all together. I loved to go into the sukkah and peek through the leaves up at the stars. Sometimes I could see the big orange harvest moon hanging in the sky. I sighed.

"I can't. Rehearsals start that Thursday."

I wouldn't even have time to help decorate the small sukkah my family puts up in our backyard.

Brad shrugged. "I gave you the message. You tell him." He loped out of the room with a handful of raisins.

"Why can't he leave me alone?" I asked, and ran upstairs.

8 CHAPTER

Everyone scrambled around the bulletin board at the studio on Tuesday to see which *Nutcracker* parts had been assigned. I had missed Monday's posting because of Rosh Hashanah. I had been home with my whole family, wishing everyone *L'shanah tovah*, a good year, and eating strudel. I had dipped lots of apples in honey and thought about how sweet this year was going to be. Wiggling my way through the crowd, I checked the list.

Fawn, of course, was Sugar Plum Fairy. The only others parts assigned were corps parts. The Waltz of the Flowers listed most of us. Snow, also, used up the class. There were no surprises. I hadn't missed much.

"I wonder who will be Dew Drop Fairy," said Janna.

"I'm hoping for Clara," said Cara. "After all, our names are practically the same."

"You're too big," Kim said. "Nadine will choose someone from the lower division."

"I can scrunch down," Cara protested.

"Why bother?" put in Jennifer. "It's hardly a dancing part. Let a little kid have it and aim for something with guts."

"Isn't anyone taking class today?" Nadine called from the studio.

We rushed in. I was glad to have something to take my mind off Ellen for a while. She was getting worse, not better. She wasn't coughing as badly, but she wasn't doing anything else either. It was as if the mere effort were too much.

The realization that we only had three months to

learn our parts and put on a professional *Nutcracker* had everyone working hard. Rehearsals were scheduled for Thursday nights and Sunday afternoons. Soon we would all know our parts and there would be costumes to be fitted and staging to perfect. It was a frantic, worried, wonderful time. Ellen would have to be better, and I would get her the best seat in the house for our premiere.

"I think we will work on bourrées today," Nadine said after we had finished our barre exercises. "A bourrée, as you know, is a tiny little moving step. When done properly, only the feet and legs move; the upper body remains still. It is an effortless appearance of floating. When improperly executed, the dancer looks clunky. She shakes and bounces. The audience should be unaware that the dancer is moving, only that she has moved. You will need to work on your bourrées for Snow. Now, let's see how you do."

Normally my dancing is fine. But let Nadine say she is focusing on one thing and it's as if I had never been taught how to do it. Bourrées were no exception. I shook. I bounced. I became Mount Saint Helens waiting to happen. So did Cara. Fawn floated. As soon as Nadine went on to something else, I floated too.

By the time class was over, the sweat was pouring down my body, dripping from my forehead, staining my leotard. Under my tights, I could feel the definition of my calf muscles—a nice, hard feel. It was a tough class. I went home feeling good.

Brad kept me company, sort of, at the table while I ate dinner. Actually, he sat there chuckling to himself about his latest Mystery Man escapade.

"It's a winner, Lys," he said. "I'm going to send it away for publication."

I sat and studied my yogurt. I'm never hungry after dancing, so I really didn't miss our family dinner. Mom used to make me eat a regular meal with the family on Hebrew school nights, but now I take yogurt and fruit salad or some of the leftovers from dinner, if they look decent. That's usually enough. I'm starved at breakfast, though. I could eat two bagels, a bowl of cereal, and a banana without stopping. And at breakfast I am not subjected to Mrs. Woonsprocket's imagination although Mom did spring Prune Spoon Muffins on us one morning. The muffin part was okay. I picked out the prunes.

It seemed as though there just weren't enough time in a day for everything. It was already eight-thirty and I still had homework. I had to begin work on my research paper for history, and my library books were due the next day. They had been sitting on my rug for two weeks, unopened. I wanted to call Ellen and tell her what Mr. Ryeback had done in class today but Mrs. Ruben wouldn't let her take any calls past eight o'clock. She said Ellen needed her rest.

I decided I should do something to cheer Ellen up instead of depressing myself. I went to my room and looked around for ideas. I spotted my Bottled Ballerina, Brad's present for my last birthday. It is a stocking stuffed with cotton sewn to look like a chubby ballerina, and then crammed into a jar. I wondered what I could make.

I went to my drawer and took out an old pair of panty hose I had been meaning to throw away because there were more runs in it than stocking. I cut off a fairly undamaged stretch of leg and stuffed it with cotton. Then I looked at it and pinched it and squashed it until it started to remind me of something—Mr. Ryeback in fact.

I got the sewing basket and found some beady little black buttons for eyes and some matted-down brown material for hair. Locating the mustache was a little harder. I finally found some snips of muddy brown yarn, which I teased with my hair brush to

make bushy. I sewed it all into place. For the final
touch, I still needed the ears. I sewed running
stitches in a semicircle on both sides of the stuffed
head until the ears started to puff out. Then I glued
wisps of yarn that I cut from the mustache into the
ears. I couldn't help laughing. It really *did* look like
Mr. Ryeback.

I ran to the kitchen and filched an old peanut
butter jar my mother was storing in the pantry and
stuffed my creation inside it. Bottled History, I
called it. If that didn't cheer up Ellen, nothing
would.

I planned to give Bottled History to Ellen the
next day, after school, but I didn't get the chance.
I stayed late to use the library and just caught the
last bus home. It was all I could do to change and
rush out the door so I wouldn't be late for ballet.
Being late for a dancing class was unprofessional.

The next couple of days were the same. I was so
busy trying to keep up with my schoolwork and
dancing that I didn't get to see Ellen until the following week after Yom Kippur. I felt a little guilty.
I made a card for her in English class to go with
Bottled History. I stopped at her house on the way
to dancing class on Thursday and rang the bell. Mrs.
Ruben opened the door almost at once.

"Oh, Alyssa. We were just leaving. We're on our way to the hospital."

"Ellen?" I said.

Mrs. Ruben stepped outside. Then I saw Ellen. She seemed to have no bones inside of her. She moved slowly and needed her mother's hand for support. She had lost weight. But, worst of all, the sparkle in her eyes was gone. She moved like a zombie. The little smile she gave me as she passed had no one behind it.

"Can I help, Mrs. Ruben?" I asked.

"If you would just pull the door closed, please, Alyssa."

I watched the two of them shuffle to the Rubens' dark blue Chevrolet. Mrs. Ruben helped Ellen into the car and then got in herself. The engine hesitated and then caught, and they pulled away. I stood there looking after them until the car disappeared around the corner. I hugged Mr. Ryeback in his peanut butter jar.

CHAPTER 9

Each day new names were posted on the bulletin board at the studio. Amy Sue got the Spanish lead. Kim got Hoops and Cara, Marzipan. I kept looking for my name, but it wasn't there yet. If I hadn't been so depressed already, I would really have been down. But all I could think of was Ellen. How could she go from having a little cold to getting pneumonia to going to the hospital in such a short time?

Dancing class dragged. I had thought rehearsal would be exciting—the first rehearsal of *The Nutcracker* has always been like walking through a door into another world for me. It didn't matter that we were still in our sweaty leotards and had just taken two-and-a-half hours of technique. What I saw in my head was a silvery world of snow with candy stripes and tinkling bells and happiness. Each rehearsal brought that world closer, so I would forget my aching calves and bleeding feet. It wouldn't matter that I had to stay up late into the night to finish my homework or that sometimes I fell asleep in the middle of a chapter and never finished my homework at all. Ballet was magic.

Only this time, the magic wasn't strong enough. When Nadine announced that the Flowers would rehearse first and the solos last, I was glad. I did not want to wait around for my part. I left as soon as Nadine dismissed the Flowers, and I headed for the hospital on my bike.

I stopped in front of the big, brick hospital building, confused. One entrance said EMERGENCY. Was Ellen an emergency or was that only for people who came in an ambulance with lights flashing and siren blaring? Another entrance said OUTPATIENT CLINIC. I had no idea what that meant. I decided that it was for people who couldn't pay. I walked up to the third entrance that said BAYLOR GENERAL HOSPITAL and pushed my way through the double glass doors.

The inside was just as confusing as the outside. People rushed here and there, disappeared into green-glassed offices, or were swallowed up by one of the red and green blinking elevators lining the center hall. I looked around, wondering what to do. I spotted an information desk and went in that direction.

"I'd like to find out what room Ellen Ruben is in, please," I said to the woman at the desk.

The woman tapped out Ellen's name into the computer.

"Her name doesn't come up on the monitor," she said. "Are you sure she was admitted?"

"I, I guess so," I stammered.

"Is she an emergency patient?"

"I don't know," I said.

"Well, when did she come in?"

"Today. I mean, this afternoon. About four-thirty."

"Oh, that explains it," she said. "Late admissions sometimes don't get entered right away if we are very busy."

The woman shuffled through some files.

"She's in room 337," she said.

"Thanks." I turned to go.

"Oh, but you can't go up," the woman told me.

"Why not?"

"Visiting hours are over. Besides, you have to be sixteen to go up to the rooms."

I hesitated only a second before saying "I *am* sixteen."

The woman gave me a crooked smile.

"Sure, you are. You can't be more than fourteen, if that."

"But she's my best friend."

"I'm sorry. That's the rule."

"Stupid rule," I muttered.

She pretended not to hear.

"Can you tell me how she is?"

"I can't give out that information. You will have to speak with her family."

"Another rule?"

The woman nodded.

"Can you at least tell me when visiting hours are?" I asked.

"Noon to eight o'clock at night."

I checked my watch. It was eight-forty-five.

"Thank you," I said, and left. I would see Ellen tomorrow, stupid rule or not.

It was dark and I had a ton of homework waiting

for me back home, but I knew I wouldn't be able to do any of it. I swung my bike around and pedaled in the opposite direction toward the synagogue, only a half mile away. Maybe they hadn't finished decorating the sukkah yet.

As soon as I turned into the parking lot, I knew I was too late. The place was mostly dark. I went inside anyway and wandered down the hall. I peeked into the sanctuary. How different it seemed without the bustle of the congregants. And how heavily quiet. It was as if the cantor's music hung in the air waiting for him to catch it in his mouth and sing it. I tiptoed out, not wanting to disturb the stillness.

The classrooms were empty except for the confirmation room, where Andy, the custodian, was sweeping the floor. He looked up when I tapped on the door, and waved.

"No use hanging around here," I whispered, and headed back the way I had come. Halfway down the corridor was the turnoff leading to the courtyard. I realized I hadn't seen the sukkah, so I took a detour and went outside.

The courtyard was cloaked in semidarkness, dimly lit by the stars and a full moon. The sukkah was in place. Leaves covered the branches that made up its roof. Someone had gotten creative and hung a harvest mobile from the center. It was a cool night. I drank in the refreshing air.

"Delightful, isn't it?"

I jumped. Rabbi Pearlman was sitting on the ground in one corner of the sukkah. In his brown suit, he blended in with the scenery. I hadn't seen him at all.

"Sorry," he said. "I didn't mean to startle you."

He got up and brushed the stray leaves and strips of bark from his pants.

"I didn't expect to see you tonight, Alyssa," he said, "but I'm glad you're here."

"Rehearsal ended early," I said.

"So did sukkah decorating. The kids came in, created a whirlwind of activity, and left just as quickly. But they did a fine job, don't you think?"

"Yes, Rabbi," I said.

"It's so peaceful here, I thought a few minutes in the courtyard might do me some good before I went home," Rabbi Pearlman continued. "Sometimes, during the holiday, I come out to relax or think things through. It's too bad we don't have a sukkah up the whole year round."

The spell of the sukkah and the rabbi's soothing voice grabbed me. I felt totally exhausted from worry

and frustration. I wanted to sit down, but there were
no chairs. If only I could rest for a minute . . .

My legs gave way, and I sank to the ground.

It was Rabbi Pearlman's turn to be startled.

"Alyssa, are you all right?" he asked.

"I'm okay," I answered. "Just tired."

He studied my face in the dim light.

"Mind if I pull up a leaf?"

I smiled as he sat down next to me. What a cartoon
this would make for Brad.

"Now, tell me. What's bothering you?"

"Nothing."

"Nothing," he said softly. "You're falling asleep
on your feet. You said you wouldn't be coming to
the synagogue to help with the sukkah but here you
are. It all sounds like something to me."

"I'm just a little worried, Rabbi."

"Worried about what?"

"About Ellen. She's in the hospital."

"Ellen Ruben? In the hospital? No one told me."

"She went in today. She has pneumonia and they
won't tell me how she's doing and I can't go up to
see her because I'm not sixteen and she's not like herself and she's my best friend and . . . and . . . I'm
scared."

I started to cry. I wanted to stop, but I couldn't.

Rabbi Pearlman took my hand and held it for a long time. Even when the tears stopped flowing and my breath came more evenly, he still held on to it, and I was glad.

"I'll tell you what," Rabbi Pearlman said after what seemed like an hour. "I'll go see her tomorrow and let you know how she is. In the meantime, I want you to go home and get some rest. By the way, how did you get here?"

"I rode my bike," I said.

"Well, we'll put your bike in the back of my car and I'll drive you home. You're in no condition to get there by yourself."

We stood up and began brushing away the leaves.

Rabbi Pearlman laughed. "I've heard of resting on your laurels, but this is ridiculous."

I couldn't help giggling. I took a deep breath and followed the rabbi to his car. Together we squeezed my bike into the back seat. He drove me home. Before he pulled away, I said, "Visiting hours are from twelve to eight, Rabbi."

"I won't forget, Alyssa," he said.

I was about to step inside my house when I heard Rabbi Pearlman beep the horn. I looked up. He waved at me and smiled. I waved back and slowly closed the door.

CHAPTER 10

Rabbi Pearlman's call came the next day just as I was about to leave for dancing.

"You're right, Alyssa," he said. "Ellen is one sick girl. But the doctors assured me that once the pneumonia is cleared up, she will return to her old self."

"I want to see her, Rabbi," I said.

"Ah, that's a little problem. The hospital is very strict about that point—they won't allow anyone under sixteen upstairs. Why don't you call Ellen on the phone?"

"She can hardly talk, Rabbi. You saw that."

"Yes, well, they say she should be out in a week and then you'll be able to see her all you like."

"Can't you take me in and say that I'm of age if they question anything? I bet they won't even ask if I'm with you."

"Are you asking me to lie, Alyssa?"

"Not lie, really, just stretch the truth a little. You said I'm an adult member of the congregation now."

"Religiously, yes," said Rabbi Pearlman, "but the hospital isn't a religious institution. I know you're trying to do the mitzvah of visiting the sick, but you'll have plenty of time for that when Ellen comes home."

I wanted to tell Rabbi Pearlman I wasn't trying to do a mitzvah at all—I just wanted to see my friend, who happened to be in the hospital. Why did everything have to be tied to Judaism?

"They must make exceptions sometimes," I persisted.

"Of course, they do, but I was told it takes something drastic for them to sidestep the rule."

"Like what?" I asked.

"Uh, like when they think the patient is about

to die. You should be glad they won't allow you in: that means Ellen is going to be all right. And I'll check on her for you, so try not to worry."

Telling someone not to worry about her best friend who is sick in the hospital is like telling an ice cube not to melt in August. I thanked Rabbi Pearlman for calling and hung up.

"I'll be a little late for dinner tonight, Mom," I said on my way out.

"Rehearsal?" Mom called after me.

I didn't answer. I just slipped Mr. Ryeback into my jacket pocket and closed the front door. Let her think I'm at rehearsal. Then she wouldn't try to stop me from sneaking in to see Ellen.

"One, and, two, and, three, and, four, and, one, and, two, and, three, and, four, and . . ."

Nadine counted out the tempo for our battements frappés at the barre.

"I want to hear you 'knock' the floor when you extend your legs. Come in sharply with your heel. Connect your heel with your ankle, Janna. Come on, come on, front-back, back-front. If you don't do doubles correctly, we'll have to go back to single and start over from Ballet One."

"What's eating her?" Cara whispered behind me.

I shrugged. With the mood Nadine was in, if I turned around to speak, she'd probably kick me out of class. She was working into her "performance personality" a bit early this year. She usually puts the pressure on about two weeks before we are due to open, yelling about how sloppy we are in our technique and how if we don't shape up, she will cancel the whole thing. We're used to it by now, but it doesn't make you feel any better when you are the one she yells at.

"I think it's because of Fawn," Cara said after class as we were unwrapping the ribbons from our pointe shoes. "Nadine is really going to miss her."

"But Nadine is the one who helped her prepare for the audition for the North Lakes Ballet and introduced her to the ballet mistress," I said.

"Yeah, but after *The Nutcracker,* Fawn will be gone. Her star will be shining somewhere else. And come next year, she'll have to choose one of us for the pas de deux and you know what she thinks about the rest of us."

I did. We all did. Not that she didn't like us or that we weren't learning and improving—we just weren't Fawn. Fawn has been with Nadine since Ballet One. Nadine molded her. Most of the rest of us came from other schools, and Nadine is always moaning about how much work she has to do to get us to unlearn all our bad habits.

"I guess we'll have to work harder, that's all," I said.

"There will be no pleasing her," grumbled Cara. "Maybe we should quit now and avoid the rush."

"Do what you want, Cara, but I'm not going to quit."

"Don't you ever wonder if it's worth it? I mean, we spend every night at the studio while our friends are doing normal things, having fun. Some of my friends don't bother inviting me to parties anymore because they know I won't be able to go. I don't want to wake up one day when I'm a senior and say 'Hey, what happened to high school?' There's a whole lot of stuff out there I haven't tried yet."

"Don't let Nadine hear you say that," I kidded. "She'd say you're being frivolous."

"I know," said Cara. "But is it frivolous to want to do more than just dance through life?"

"That's all *I* want to do," I said as I packed my gear, grabbed my jacket, and rose to leave.

"Want to go to the newsstand and get some Italian ices?" asked Cara.

"I can't. I have to go someplace."

"See. You *have* another life. Where is *my* other life?"

I left her there on the floor. As I unchained my bike from the rail, I thought about what Cara had said. I was trying to get rid of my "other life" while she was trying to get into one. It would have been so much easier if we could have switched places.

I glanced at my watch to make sure I wouldn't get to the hospital after visiting hours. It was twenty-five minutes before eight. I sped down the road, thankful the hospital was only five minutes away.

I parked my bike alongside the hospital fence. There was no question about which door to use this time. I peeked through the glass doors, looking for the woman at the information desk. I would have to get around her some way. But she wasn't there. A man was sitting at the desk, reading a newspaper. I pushed open the doors and walked inside past the desk. I was halfway to the elevators when he called out to me.

"Oh, miss. Where are you going?"

"To the elevators," I answered.

"I'm sorry. Children are not allowed upstairs."

Children! At least the woman had thought I looked fourteen.

"I'm waiting for someone to come down," I said. I didn't mind a little truth stretching even if Rabbi Pearlman did. I actually was waiting for someone to come down . . . so I could get into the empty elevator and go up!

"Okay," said the man. He went back to reading his newspaper.

A minute later an elevator opened its doors. I entered quickly and pressed number three. I was on my way up. If only I could get to Ellen's room without being seen.

The elevator opened to a stream of waiting people. I dodged between them and eased past the nurses' desk, following the arrow pointing the way to rooms 325 to 340. Room 337 was at the end of the hall. I hurried as fast as I dared without attracting attention to myself and slipped into Ellen's room.

Ellen turned toward the doorway as I entered. I was shocked when I saw her. She had a plastic oxygen mask covering her mouth and nose, which made me think of all the movies I had seen where the hero didn't make it. It was her eyes, though, those beautiful, lively eyes, that really shook me. They were dull, sunken.

"Ellen?" I whispered.

She took off the mask and said, "Come on in, Alyssa."

I walked over to her bed and stood there not knowing what to say.

Ellen smiled a weak little smile.

"Having pneumonia is the pits," she said.

"How are you doing?" I asked.

"Better. That's what my doctor tells me, but I'm not so sure. I'm fed up with being in bed, and I'm too tired to do anything else."

It took her a while to get out the sentence. Talking seemed to make her weaker.

"I brought you something," I said.

I reached into my jacket and pulled out Mr. Ryeback.

"Here."

Ellen took the jar.

"Is that . . . ?"

I nodded.

"It's great. Ear hairs and all."

"I wanted to give it to you yesterday, but you were just leaving when I got to your house."

"That's okay. I wouldn't have been able to appreciate it yesterday anyway."

Ellen took a few panting breaths. She put Bottled

History on the small table next to her bed and fumbled for the mask. I helped her put it on.

Bells sounded and a voice said softly over the public address system: "Visiting hours are over."

"I'd better go," I told Ellen. "I'll get in trouble if they catch me here. I'm not sixteen, you know."

Ellen waved feebly.

I edged my way to the door.

"I'll try to come tomorrow."

Ellen blinked and tried to smile but wasn't very successful at it.

The trip to the elevator on the way down was easier. I just squeezed in with a group of people in the hall, and we traveled down together.

As I walked past the man at the information desk, he looked up from his paper and said, "Found who you were waiting for?"

I stared at him blankly for a minute. I didn't know what he was talking about; then I remembered what I had told him. It seemed so long ago.

"Yes," I said. "They're outside already. I'd better hurry."

I rushed out. It was kind of fun, fooling him that way. I would have to tell Ellen about it. Maybe it would make her laugh. I hoped something would.

11 CHAPTER

On Saturday, I brought Ellen a piece of strudel, foil-wrapped and decorated with a bright purple bow. I also brought along a book called *Sweet Success*, which was a sequel to the book *Success Story* Ellen had been reading before she got sick. It was a good thing my jacket had big pockets.

Outside the hospital, I latched onto the end of a family loaded down with gifts trailing pink curlicued ribbon. Two little girls who couldn't have been more than eight or ten were holding pink-papered packages. They were laughing and happy, and I realized they must be visiting someone who just had a baby. I took out my strudel and trailed after them, sailing past the information desk as if I belonged.

In the elevator, I waited until they got off before pushing the button for Ellen's floor. Saturday at a hospital is a busy place, and I had no trouble reaching Ellen's room unnoticed.

"Hi," I called softly as I entered.

Ellen had been lying on her bed staring at a blank television screen.

"Do you want me to turn it on?" I asked.

"No," she replied, and continued to stare.

"I brought you some of my grandmother's famous strudel, famous in the Stein family anyway."

I put the little package on her night table.

"Thanks."

"And here's the next book about Success."

I took it from my pocket and placed it on the bed near her.

"Thanks," she said again.

Ellen didn't move to pick it up.

"Um, I forgot to tell you what happened at school yesterday. We had a fire drill in the middle of math while we were taking a test, and no one wanted to leave, but they made us because there was a real fire this time. It started in the trash bin outside the cafeteria, and the fire department was called. We stood outside for half an hour while they checked through the school to make sure everything was okay. By then, math was over and we had to turn in our incomplete tests and Ms. Wilson is mad because she has to make up a whole new test for us."

"I would have failed anyway," Ellen said.

"Not with me helping you, you wouldn't."

"I'm going to fail everything this year," Ellen went on.

"What are you talking about? You'll get out of here, and I'll help you catch up with the work."

Ellen sighed a long, drawn-out sigh.

"That's all right, Lyssa. I don't care if I fail. It doesn't matter."

"Of course it matters. I'm not going to ninth grade without you."

"I'm too tired. I just want to sleep."

"Well, this is the place to do it."

"Not really. There are people always coming and going or waking you for tests. And my mother keeps calling on the phone."

The flatness of her voice frightened me. I had

never heard Ellen sound like that. She is the one who always tries to cheer me up when I'm depressed, mostly about dancing. I sometimes wonder if she has ginger ale in her veins instead of blood because she is so bubbly all the time.

"Young lady, what are you doing here?"

The floor nurse had discovered me.

"I came to visit my friend," I said.

"I can see that, but how did you get in? Don't you know you cannot come upstairs unless you are sixteen or older?"

"I saw a whole family with young children get into the elevator, so I did too," I said.

"They were going to the maternity floor. Families are allowed there but not here. You will have to leave."

"But my friend needs me," I said.

"She is well taken care of by hospital personnel."

How could I tell her there were times when nurses and doctors and medicine weren't the only things a sick person needed. I knew my friend a lot better than they did, and I wasn't happy about what I was seeing.

She stood at the door, waiting, a soldier guarding the fort.

"I have to go, Ellen," I said disgustedly. "Take care of yourself."

The nurse stepped aside, barely, to let me pass and watched as I made my way across the hall to the bank of elevators. She didn't take her eyes off me until I was inside one of them on my way down.

"You should see her, Mom. It's like there's no one home." My mother was getting ready to go out for the evening.

"That sounds like an exaggeration, Alyssa."

"But it isn't. Have you ever known Ellen not to care about something, anything, especially her schoolwork? She thinks she is going to fail and she doesn't care!"

"She's sick, Lyssa. You don't want to do anything either when you're sick in bed. Give her a few days. She'll feel better and start phoning, and the two of you will be planning your next outing."

"I hope you're right, Mom."

"Listen to an ex-nurse."

"Why did you stop being a nurse, Mom?" I asked. It was something I had always wondered about and somehow never seemed to get around to asking.

"Other things came along in my life—like you and Brad."

"You could have gone back to nursing when we grew up. Didn't you like it?"

Mom stopped fussing and stared thoughtfully into the mirror.

"Didn't I like it? Yes, I liked nursing. I also liked mothering and housekeeping. I especially liked cooking. It was a creative outlet for me when you kids were driving me nuts. So when the opportunity came to cook and get paid for it, I decided to change careers. Hand me that necklace, please, Lyssa."

I reached for the beaded necklace Mom pointed to. Mom took it and fastened it around her neck, patting it into place.

"Were you any good as a nurse?" I asked.

"I thought so. So did my supervisor at nursing school, who recommended me for my first job. What is this sudden interest in nursing?"

I plopped down on Mom's bed.

"What I don't understand is, if you planned to be a nurse all your life, how could you just stop being one?"

"People are complex creatures, Lyssa. They are able to be interested in many things at once."

"Not with dancing you can't be," I said.

"Even with dancing. You still are a person and have human needs."

"But they always tell you you have to give up everything to be a great dancer, Mom."

"If you choose to," Mom said. "There are very few Makarovas, Alyssa. Even Nadine Perrin has a life outside of the dance studio."

She bent to kiss me.

"You don't have to feel like a traitor if you want to explore different things in life." She turned around. "How do I look?"

"Nice," I said.

Mom smiled. "We can discuss this further at another time if you'd like, but I really have to run. I'm meeting Daddy in town for dinner before the play. Brad said the two of you could handle dinner for yourselves."

"Have a good time," I said.

The instant she left, Brad came bounding up the stairs.

"On your feet, lazy. Look what I have."

He held up a manila folder filled with papers. Mom's recipe folder!

"We're going to surprise Mom and test out one of these weirdo concoctions."

"She'll kill us!" I protested.

"Nah, she won't."

He yanked me from the bed. I stumbled down the stairs after him, catching his excitement.

"Here. You take half the pile and I'll take the other half."

"What am I looking for?"

"Anything edible. A recipe by Mrs. Woonsprocket is automatically disqualified."

We searched through appetizers, salads, entrées, desserts.

"How about this?" I said. "Tiny Tuna Turnovers."

"Who sent it in?" asked Brad.

I checked the name. "Mrs. Annie Bahdee."

"Would *you* eat something made by someone with that name?"

"What's wrong with it? Anybody can have a funny name . . . anybody . . . Oh, I get it—Annie Bahdee—anybody!"

I started laughing. Brad grinned. Then he started laughing too. Before we knew it we were holding onto the kitchen chairs so we wouldn't fall to the floor. I tossed the recipe into the air, and that got us hysterical again.

"We'll never eat supper at this rate," I gasped.

"Right," panted Brad.

We took a couple of deep breaths and went on with our search.

Brad came up with "Yam Yum Tum Tum."

"You have to eat that while beating a drum. No good."

We finally agreed to try Mystery Meatpie, only we didn't have chopped beef, so we used leftover chicken and we substituted zucchini for (ugh) okra. It didn't taste bad. In fact, with some mushroom sauce, it was pretty good. The only thing was that even though we had used a frozen pie shell, it still looked kind of lopsided.

"Let's leave some for Mom to taste," I said, as I reached for the dish and took some more.

"This should give Mrs. Woonsprocket a challenge," said Brad, taking a second helping.

"You know, Brad, you should make Mystery Meatpie Mystery Man's favorite food."

Brad bolted straight up in his chair. "That's a great idea. Mystery Man creates a new, exciting dinner every night. He stirs together whatever he has around to eat so it's always something unknown, just as his identity is unknown. The perfect mystery dish for the perfect mystery person! I'd better get this down before I forget."

Brad jumped out of his chair and ran into his room, and I was left to clean up. For once, I didn't mind. Clearing away the dinner dishes gave me time to think. I knew Mom was wrong about Ellen. She wasn't going to bounce back so easily. I'd help as much as I could, of course, but I wouldn't have much time. If only she hadn't gotten sick before *The Nutcracker.*

12 CHAPTER

Ellen came home on Tuesday. At least her body did; she was somewhere else.

I went straight to her house after school.

"So. How does it feel to be home again?" I asked.

The usual answer to an obvious question like that was "great," but that wasn't what Ellen said. She kind of looked up at me from her slumped-in-bed position and said, "What does it matter? Here or there—it's just the same."

"Come on, Ellen, snap out of it," I demanded.

"You don't know," she said. "First the pain, then the trouble breathing. You just want it all to stop, but it keeps on until you feel you'll never get better, so why even try."

"But the doctor said you'll get better. Look, you're better now, or they wouldn't have let you leave the hospital."

"They needed the bed," said Ellen.

Nothing I said seemed to help. I was glad when Mrs. Ruben came in with a tray of soup and crackers.

"Snack time," Mrs. Ruben sang out.

"I don't want any," Ellen said.

"Sure, you do, honey. You need to build up your strength."

"I said I don't want it."

Mrs. Ruben glanced at me and then put the tray on Ellen's night table.

"I'll leave it here in case you change your mind."

"I don't care," said Ellen.

"I wish you cared about something, Ellen," Mrs. Ruben said. "At least try reading; you always liked to read."

"It gives me a headache. I can't concentrate."

Ellen rolled over in bed and faced away from her mother.

Mrs. Ruben sighed and went out.

I had been standing nervously at the edge of Ellen's bed not knowing what to do or say. Now I decided that what I did wasn't important as long as I got Ellen interested in something.

"Hey, El," I said. "I think I might have a party next weekend. I'll have a few of the gang over and you, of course, and maybe we'll make some really different ice cream sundaes. Remember the time we tried to convince our parents that ice cream made a nutritious lunch, so we threw in raw carrots and raisins and anything else we thought would sucker them in?" I laughed at the memory. "We each took a spoonful, and then we threw the whole thing in the garbage."

"Yeah, I remember," she said. She turned over again and smiled that weak little smile.

"So you'll come?" I said hopefully.

"No."

"Why not?"

"I'm just too tired."

"Don't worry. In a week, you'll have some of your energy back."

"Sorry, Lyssa, but I don't feel like going to a party, now or a week from now."

Before I had a chance to argue with her, Ellen said, "Isn't it almost time for dancing?"

"Ellen . . ."

"You'll be late if you don't hurry."

"I'll see you tomorrow?"

"If you want."

I left Ellen staring at the wall the way she had stared at the blank television screen in the hospital. So much for my brilliant scheme. While I don't like to tell parents too much, I knew I would have to tell Mrs. Ruben about Ellen's reaction to the party idea. In all the years I've known Ellen, she has never *not* wanted to go to a party. Even when she had the flu, Ellen was ready to get out of bed to go to a school dance.

Mrs. Ruben was in the hallway and grabbed my arm as I came out of Ellen's room.

"Alyssa," she said, "I must talk to you."

She led me to the kitchen.

"Would you like a drink or a piece of fruit, Alyssa?"

"No, thank you, Mrs. Ruben," I said.

"Well, then I'll get right to the point. You see how Ellen is. I'm worried about her. She's pulling

away from us. She won't talk to me or to Mr.
Ruben. She doesn't want to do any of the things
she usually enjoys. I don't want to push her to do
her schoolwork yet, but she isn't interested in that
either. You're her best friend, Alyssa. Can you
help?"

I fidgeted with my watchband, twisting it around
on my wrist. I couldn't tell Mrs. Ruben about the
party now. It would only worry her more.

"How can I help?" I asked.

"That's the problem," Mrs. Ruben said. "I don't
really know. What I *do* know is that we must get
Ellen back to her old self."

Back to the land of the living, I thought.

"Maybe she'll let me help her with her math," I
said. "That's what she has the most trouble with in
school, so she might not want to get too far behind
in it."

"That's an excellent idea, Alyssa. She goes to
sleep early, so come at this time. Oh, I do hope it
works."

I checked my watch. It was a little after four. I
didn't have the heart to tell Mrs. Ruben I had to go
to dancing now. After all, what was dancing com-
pared with helping Ellen? And yet it was less than
a month since I had started full-time, and I really

hated to miss a class. I was thankful that tomorrow was only Wednesday. Rehearsal was Thursday, and I couldn't miss that.

The final postings were made for *The Nutcracker.* I was cast for two corps parts—Waltz of the Flowers and Snow—and I was the Soldier Doll. It wasn't the Dew Drop Fairy, which had gone to Janna, but it was a solo and a nice one.

"Oh, no, look who has Clara," Amy Sue moaned.

The part of Clara had been assigned to a girl in the lower level. Last year she had been one of the girls in the party scene. She had worn a forest-green satin dress with pink and green ribbons in her long blond hair. She looked so sweet, it was hard to believe how pushy she was. She wormed her way into the rehearsal room and took warm-up barre with the professional division students. Nadine thought it was cute. We thought it was obnoxious.

"I still think I should be Clara," Cara grumbled.

"Come on, Cara," said Amy Sue. "You know you're too big. They would have to make a whole new costume for you."

"I guess I wouldn't mind so much if it had gone to almost anyone else."

"But Nadine loves her. She was in the little kids' creative dance class and is working her way up in the school," I said.

We stopped talking. It was the Fawn story all over again except that Fawn was a nicer person. We were thinking about it when Nadine called us to class.

I worked my toes off. Nadine said we had to take class on pointe from now on to build up our strength. We usually wear our slippers during most of the class and switch to pointe for the last half hour. Once a week we have partnering, which is all on pointe.

Dancing on pointe is hard. The whole body is balanced on the tips of the dancer's feet—sometimes on only one foot and then only on the toes that actually hit the floor, usually the first three. You have to concentrate because it is easy to lose your balance and come crashing down or get hurt.

Just as we were about to break class, Nadine called us together.

"I am making some changes in the dances this year," she said, "so there will be additional rehearsals. Starting tomorrow, we will rehearse on Wednesdays as well as Thursdays and Sundays."

I felt my stomach drop. I groaned.

"Do you have a problem, Alyssa?" Nadine asked.

Boy, did I have a problem. I had promised Mrs. Ruben I would help Ellen. I could tell her something had come up and I'd be there the next day. No, that was Thursday and another rehearsal. Either I'd miss a rehearsal and help Ellen tomorrow or I'd go to rehearsal and feel rotten for not helping my best friend when she needed me most.

As much as I wanted to say no, there's no problem, I'll be here tomorrow, I couldn't back out on Ellen.

"I can't come tomorrow," I said. "I didn't know there would be rehearsal and I . . . I can't come. I won't even be in class."

Nadine's eyebrow arched up.

"Is there anyone else who can't make it?"

We all looked around the room at one another. No one else raised her hand.

"Sorry, Alyssa," said Nadine, "everyone else can come. This will count as one absence. Remember, if you miss three rehearsals, I will have to give your parts to someone else."

"That's too bad," said Cara in the dressing room.

Well, I consoled myself, it was only one rehearsal. I just wouldn't miss any more.

13 CHAPTER

I discovered one thing about math—you can't make someone understand it if that person isn't paying attention. Ellen didn't even want to open the book.

"It's easy, El," I coaxed. "I'll teach it to you so you won't be behind when you get back to school."

"I'll be behind anyway, so don't bother," Ellen said.

"It isn't a bother. I *want* to do it. This way I get to spend some time with you."

I *did* want to be with Ellen, but I was having a hard time paying attention too. My mind was half on Ellen and half on dancing. We would have been at the end of the barre by now, I thought. My feet automatically pointed. I could feel my calf muscles tense. Ellen must have picked up my feelings.

"Go to dancing, Lyssa," she said.

"If I wanted to go to dancing, I would," I said guiltily. "Right now I want to teach you math."

We got through one page, but I could tell nothing was sinking in.

"Please, Ellen, try," I said.

"Maybe tomorrow," she said. "I'm tired. I think I'll go to sleep. You don't mind, do you, Lys?"

Ellen shut off the light by her bed and closed her eyes. There was nothing I could do but leave. Mrs. Ruben was waiting for me downstairs.

"Well?" she asked.

"We worked on one page," I said. I didn't tell her we might as well have been playing basketball for all Ellen had learned.

"Oh, good. You'll come again tomorrow?"

"I can come after school, Mrs. Ruben, but I can't stay long. I have rehearsal and I need to be there."

"As long as you come, Alyssa," Mrs. Ruben said. "Ellen counts on you so much; we all do."

I almost told her that Ellen practically threw me out. I wanted to say I had other important things to do, that it was *her* job to take care of Ellen, not mine. But I couldn't say any of it. I just tied up the words and swallowed them. They landed in my stomach in a tight little knot and stayed there. I said good-bye to Mrs. Ruben.

"Good-bye, and Alyssa . . . thank you."

I stood outside the Rubens' door wondering what to do. It was only five-thirty. Maybe if I hurried and changed, I could make rehearsal after all. Then I realized that with all the fuss I had caused yesterday, I would be too embarrassed to show up now. Anyway, my dancing would be bad. I hadn't warmed up. I could go home, but then I'd end up eating Chickpea Croquettes, a vegetarian delight submitted by M. Goldfarb of Toronto, Canada.

I decided that some ice cream would make me feel better. As I biked down to the store, I convinced myself that an ice cream soda was less fattening than a sundae. I sat at the counter and ordered a black and white.

I made the soda last a long time. I hoped the

longer it took, the less upset I would be, but with each sip I thought about Ellen. Why was she like that? What could I do? She didn't want my help, anyway, so why should I keep trying?

What I really needed to do was talk to someone about the situation. I couldn't talk to Mrs. Ruben— she made me feel uncomfortable. Besides, she didn't know what to do any more than I did. Mom kept telling me to wait, that when Ellen's body got better, so would Ellen's spirit. But then, she hadn't seen Ellen. The only other person who might understand was Rabbi Pearlman. He had seen her. Maybe he could help. Then I'd be able to concentrate on my dancing.

Once again, I headed for the synagogue. This time, the lights blazed throughout the building. I had forgotten it was Wednesday and classes were still going on. I knew where to find the rabbi; he taught the confirmation class. I peeked into the room, trying to see the wall clock so I would know how much longer I would have to wait until class ended. It was seven-thirty. The class ended at eight. Rabbi Pearlman noticed me and waved me inside. I slipped into a seat in back.

"So, where were we? Brian?"

"Working our way through the mitzvot," said

the boy sitting next to me. He rolled his eyes. "All six hundred thirteen of them." Everybody laughed.

"Yes, the mitzvot," said Rabbi Pearlman. "Is it possible to do them all, was the question. And if you don't, are you still a good Jew?"

"There are some we can't do, Rabbi," said a girl. "How can you leave the corners of your field unharvested if you don't have a field?"

"Well, how can you?" Rabbi Pearlman asked the group. "Remember, the mitzvot are not just good deeds but imply some sense of obligation. Yes, Rachel?"

"Maybe it just means you shouldn't take everything for yourself, that you should leave some of what you have for those who don't have anything," she said. "Then it wouldn't matter if you gave part of your crop or volunteered time at an old people's home or donated money to charity. It would still be sharing."

There was a murmur of understanding.

"What do you do if you want to follow a mitzvah, but there are obstacles put in your way to prevent you from doing so?" asked Rabbi Pearlman.

"I would find a way around the obstacles," someone said.

"I know of someone who did that," the rabbi said. "When she went to visit a sick friend in the hospital and was told she was not allowed up because she was underage, she sneaked in. What do you think about that?"

"It wasn't very honest," said Brian. "The hospital probably had good reasons for making that rule."

"But she did perform a mitzvah," Rachel said.

My face reddened as I tried to scrunch down in my seat. So he had known all the time. If Rabbi Pearlman said who that person was, I would never forgive him. But the conversation went in a different direction.

"Think about this," he continued. "What if you are your own obstacle. What if you know what the Jewish thing to do would be, but you choose a different path. Assuming you don't hurt anyone in the process, are you less of a Jew if you follow only those teachings that fit in with your personal needs?"

"Yes."

"No."

"I hear some difference of opinion. Let's take a little poll."

Hands were raised and votes counted. The class was split in its vote. There was a large "I don't know" vote. If I had voted, I would have fallen into that category. I felt Jewish inside, but I still didn't know how much had to show on the outside.

"That's something we can discuss next week," said Rabbi Pearlman.

I looked up at the clock. It was eight o'clock already. A half hour had flown by. I couldn't believe it.

Rabbi Pearlman stopped by my seat as the class was packing up to go.

"Did you want to see me, Alyssa?" he asked.

"It's about Ellen," I said.

He nodded. "I thought it might be. How can I help?"

"That's just what I came to ask you, Rabbi. I don't know what to do. Ellen just lies there like a lump, and I can't perk her up. Today I tried to get her thinking about schoolwork, but she couldn't care less. Mrs. Ruben thinks I can help get her back to normal, but I don't know if I can. I've tried, but I can't even make her laugh."

"You mean Bottled History?" said Rabbi Pearlman. "I laughed. I didn't know you were so artistic."

"I'm not really. I took the idea from a birthday

present I got last year." I blushed again. Rabbi Pearlman didn't miss a thing.

"Maybe someday if you have some spare time,
although I know you are busy with your dancing,
I wouldn't mind if you stuffed me into a bottle."

The image of Rabbi Pearlman in a peanut butter
jar was too funny to keep inside. I laughed aloud.
He laughed too.

"That sounds wonderful, Alyssa. Did you ever
hear the expression 'Laughter is the best medicine'?
That goes for the sick as well as the sick at heart."

"That's what my grandma says. But, Rabbi,
Ellen won't laugh."

"Not at the moment, perhaps, but you'll find a
way."

"That's part of the problem, Rabbi. I don't have
time to find a way. I have dancing every day and
rehearsals three times a week. I've already missed
one rehearsal; if I miss two more I won't be in *The
Nutcracker*. But Mrs. Ruben keeps begging me to
help. I'm only a kid. What does she expect of me?
I don't know what to do."

"What can I say, Alyssa? Life is full of tough
decisions."

"But I don't have a choice," I wailed. "I can't be
kicked out of *The Nutcracker!*"

"Of course you have a choice," said Rabbi Pearl-man. "You can help or not. Ellen will get better with or without your help."

I sighed. I had come to the synagogue so Rabbi Pearlman could tell me that I had done enough and I could go back to thinking only about dancing. He wasn't doing it.

"But you think Ellen might get well sooner with my help?" I asked.

"Who knows?" said Rabbi Pearlman.

I got up and walked around the classroom. There were maps of Israel taped to the back wall. American and Israeli flags hung in front of the room. Strung along the length of the room was a line with snap-shots clothespinned to it. They were photos of members of the confirmation class laughing, holding hands, working together. Ellen and I had laughed, held hands, worked together.

It wasn't fair. Then I thought of the discussion about the field. I had harvested all these years of Ellen's friendship; surely I could leave the corners of the field for her to harvest now.

Someone had written SMILE on the chalkboard in Hebrew. I smiled and turned back to Rabbi Pearl-man.

"Ellen likes to read," I told him, "but she hasn't even opened the book I brought her, and it's about one of her favorite characters."

"Maybe reading takes too much effort. Remember, she's still weak. What else does she enjoy?"

"Singing," I said. How could I have forgotten? At every party, Ellen organizes a singing group. She is in the chorus at school. She's always singing with the radio.

"Well, she probably won't be able to sing yet," said the rabbi.

"No, but she can listen. That doesn't take too much effort. I know her favorite singers and the songs she likes. I can bring some tapes over and play them for her."

"It's certainly worth a try. Oh, that reminds me," said Rabbi Pearlman. "We have Ellen's bat mitzvah tape in the office. Would you bring it to her?"

"Yes," I said. It wasn't exactly the kind of singing I had in mind for Ellen, but I would take it over anyway.

I trailed Rabbi Pearlman down the hall to the synagogue office. He opened the file cabinet and took out a manila folder with a cassette in it.

"This is Ellen's portion for her bat mitzvah," he

said. "Mrs. Hershkowitz will help her with it when she is better, but I thought she might want to have it now."

I said good-bye to Rabbi Pearlman and went outside. The air was crisp and clean. The stars sparkled with a sharp, bright light. With a quick look back at the now-dark synagogue, I left, thinking about how Rabbi Pearlman's pudgy cheeks and crinkly, laughing eyes would be easy to make out of stockings. I'd call it Jarred Judaism.

CHAPTER 14

I stopped by Ellen's house Thursday after school to bring her the bat mitzvah tape and three cassettes by her favorite singers.

"I brought you the latest ones, El," I said. "The ones we went crazy trying to find at the mall last month."

Ellen lay motionless on her bed, as usual. I could

see it was going to be a fight to get her out of the blahs.

"You'll never guess where I finally found them."

Ellen didn't say a word.

"Well?" I said.

"Well, what?" Ellen asked.

"Guess."

"You said I wouldn't be able to."

"Since when did that stop you from trying?"

"I don't know, Lys."

"Guess anyway," I insisted. If I had to work at it, so would she.

"Crayhall's Music Store," Ellen said with little enthusiasm.

"Nope. Guess again."

"Eastwind Video."

"Wrong. It was Meyerhoff's Drugstore. Isn't that a weird place to find music? I went in for waterproof tape to wrap around my toes for pointe and the cassettes were sitting there in a wire basket near the cash register. I never did get what I went in for. I only had enough money for one or the other. I'll wrap my toes with tissues instead."

Ellen gave me that stupid little smile again. Why couldn't she laugh? Or cry? Or something?

"I'll put one in your tape machine. Which do you want to hear first?"

"It doesn't matter."

"Well, then, pick one," I said, tossing them on her bed. Ellen reached out and touched one of the tapes. I put it on and adjusted the volume.

I listened to it for about ten minutes with her and then I had to go.

"I don't know if I'll get to see you before next week, El," I said as I was getting ready to leave. "I have rehearsals at night and I have to research my history paper or I'm dead."

"Okay," said Ellen.

"Bye," I called from the doorway.

"Bye."

I hoped I could leave quietly so Mrs. Ruben wouldn't catch me in the hall, but she was waiting at the bottom of the stairs.

"How did it go today?" she asked.

"About the same," I answered. Mrs. Ruben bit her lip.

I didn't want to depress her, but I couldn't help it. Ellen just wasn't coming out of it. She had to know. I hoped the music would help.

When I left, Mrs. Ruben was staring up the stairs.

I was looking forward to ballet class. I was going to work so hard, the sweat would drip down my forehead into my eyes. Every muscle would be ready for rehearsal. My body tingled at the thought as if it had already started its workout.

"Yeah!" I said aloud.

Before I got my foot on the pedal of my bike, Mrs. Ruben came running outside. For a split second I was tempted to pretend I didn't see her and take off at top speed. It was her voice that stopped me. She sounded helpless, calling my name as she ran and begging me to stay. For Ellen's sake. I followed her back inside, my body aching worse than it would have from class. This was the second rehearsal missed. I prayed Nadine would understand. I didn't hold out much hope.

Sunday at the dance studio was a madhouse. The costumes were in. The place was a fluff of white netting, boxes, and plastic bags.

"Look, look, look!" shouted Amy Sue. She held up a coffee-colored costume for the Spanish lead. She twirled and stamped her feet and snapped her fingers.

"Where are the castanets?"

"Props aren't in yet, Amy Sue," said Nadine,

who was watching all the excitement. "Take it easy with the costume."

"Sorry," Amy Sue said, embarrassed.

"We will have final fittings for as many costumes as possible during rehearsal today, girls. Jennifer's mother will be helping. She will be calling you out one by one as the rest of us work. There are two things to remember about the costumes; they are to be treated carefully and kept clean, and you must control your appetites after the fitting. Final fitting means just that—final. If you grow out of your costume, you have to fix it."

I held in my stomach. Until *The Nutcracker*, I wouldn't even *think* of fattening foods. There would be no doughnuts, no banana cream pie, no ice cream sundaes. I groaned, remembering the soda I had had last week. The only compensation was that Mom wouldn't force me to try tonight's specialty— Creamed Rhubarb Rhapsody.

Nadine was working with me on my Soldier Doll part when Jennifer's mom came into the studio.

"There's a phone call for you, Alyssa."

Nadine did not approve of private phone calls, coming in or going out, especially during a working session. I was not expecting one. I looked at Nadine. She waggled her hand at me and went to work with

Kim. I went to the desk in the outer room and picked up the phone.

"Hello?"

"Oh, Alyssa, I'm so glad you're there," said the voice. "This is Mrs. Ruben."

Oh, no, I thought. Two missed rehearsals and now she was calling me at the studio. Well, I would just have to tell her I'm sorry, Mrs. Ruben, I can't help today. With my mind made up, I cleared my throat and spoke as calmly as I could into the phone.

"Is Ellen all right, Mrs. Ruben?" I asked. When Ellen's mother got nervous, it took forever to get a story out of her. I wanted to know the end before she got started.

"Well, yes and no," she said. "I mean, her body is all right, but she isn't responding to me. After you left on Thursday, I went in to see how she was feeling and I found her lying in the same position in bed, not moving, with the tape machine still on. I assumed she was just tired from your visit, so I shut it off and turned off her light. But she's been like that ever since. She eats a little, sleeps a little, talks in one-word sentences. This morning, I asked her a question, but she didn't answer at all. I was so scared, I shouted at her and then she looked at me but, but, she didn't seem *there*. Alyssa, can you come right over?"

"I'm in the middle of rehearsal, Mrs. Ruben. Why don't you call Ellen's doctor?"

"I did, but all I got was the answering service, and no one has called back yet."

"Is Mr. Ruben . . . ?"

"Mr. Ruben isn't home and I don't know where to reach him. Oh . . . Oh . . . ."

Then Mrs. Ruben began to cry.

Don't go, I told myself. Ellen will be okay. Mrs. Ruben is just upset. It's probably not as bad as she thinks. But in my guts I knew what I would say.

"I'll be right there, Mrs. Ruben," I said and hung up.

I threw my pink slippers into my bag and pulled on my jeans. I interrupted Kim and told Nadine I had to go.

"That's three, Alyssa," she said. "You know what that means."

"I know," I murmured, barely able to force out the words.

I sped along Morrisey Street. I spun around Ellen's corner and pulled up in front of her house. Mrs. Ruben must have been watching from the window because the door opened as soon as I stepped up to it.

"I'm sorry for bothering you, Alyssa, but I didn't know what else to do."

I took a deep breath before speaking.

"That's okay, Mrs. Ruben. Ellen's my best friend."

We went upstairs. I looked at Ellen. She didn't look back.

"See?" said Mrs. Ruben.

"Come on, El," I said in my most cheerful voice. She fluttered her eyelids, but that was all. Mrs. Ruben stuffed her fist into her mouth and whimpered.

"Could I please have something to drink, Mrs. Ruben?" I asked.

"Orange juice?" she said.

"How about hot chocolate?" It would take longer to prepare. I wanted to keep her out of the room for a little while. She was making me very nervous. When she left, I went over to Ellen.

"You're my best friend, right?" I said.

Ellen nodded slowly.

"Then, you have to let me help you. You don't want to do math. That's okay. You don't have to read. But you have to let me know you're here. Please, El. I need you. Don't pull away from me."

Ellen took a deep breath but didn't say anything.

"Tell you what. I'm going to put on one of the tapes, and we'll listen to it together."

I picked out the one with the loudest, fastest music and put it on. You couldn't help feeling the beat. It had to get some response from Ellen.

Halfway through side one, I gave up on it. I fed another tape into the machine. I watched closely for a change of expression on Ellen's face, but there wasn't any. I took it out and stuffed a third tape in. Now I was mad. I had left rehearsal and would be kicked out of *The Nutcracker* for nothing. She wasn't even trying.

The tape started. I was surprised. I had expected to hear the blasting sounds of a rock record. Instead, I had put in the bat mitzvah tape. The familiar Hebrew chants sang out into the room. I was about to remove the tape when I heard a sound from Ellen.

"Are you all right, El?" I asked as I turned. I started toward the bed and stopped in my tracks. I just stood there, staring. Tears were trickling down Ellen's cheeks. The sound I had heard was a sob.

"Oh, El," I finally managed to say.

Ellen reached out her arms, and I ran to them. Crying and laughing, we rocked back and forth together on the bed.

"Thanks," whispered Ellen.

We sat and listened together as the tape played on. The haunting tones seemed to be blessing us.

Mrs. Ruben entered with a mug of steaming hot chocolate. When she saw Ellen, her face dissolved into a waterfall of tears. I moved out of the way and took the mug from her hands as she rushed to her daughter.

"My baby, my baby," Mrs. Ruben said over and over as she held Ellen tightly.

I took the untasted hot chocolate down to the kitchen. How confusing things were. I had tried to get Ellen interested in school, in music, in reading, in funny stories, but nothing had worked. The last thing I expected was a reaction to the bat mitzvah tape. I had not listened to mine since my bat mitzvah. I suddenly wanted to go home and listen to it; I was going to need some comfort after what I had done today.

Mom and Dad were surprised to see me home so early. I saw Mom's questioning look. I desperately wanted to tell her about Ellen and Mrs. Ruben and dancing, but the words wouldn't come out.

Every time I thought about missing the ballet, I felt sick. I mumbled something about having a headache and went to my room. I was so glad that Ellen, at last, had started to come alive. Now she would get well. But, oh, not to be in *The Nutcracker*. I grabbed my pillow and buried my face in it. It was my turn to cry.

15 CHAPTER

The bulletin board at dancing told the story Monday. My name was crossed off as the Soldier Doll and replaced by Maureen's, a girl from the corps. I had known it would happen and yet I kept hoping nothing would change, that Nadine didn't really mean it. My eyes misted over. I pretended to be studying the soda machine when Amy Sue walked in.

"Hey, Alyssa," she called. "Someone crossed off your name on the assignment sheet. Nadine will be furious."

Amy Sue had a knack for being clumsy in many ways. I choked back the tears and answered her.

"No, she won't," I said. "I had to miss three rehearsals, so I'm out."

"Oh," she said.

Just then Cara came in. Amy Sue dragged her into the studio. I knew what they would be talking about, but I didn't care. Soon the whole school would be talking about it. I thought about leaving and never coming back, at least until *The Nutcracker* was over, but then I would be punished twice—once by not being in the ballet and then by having my body fall to pieces by not going to class. I stayed.

Each day before class I went to visit Ellen. She was getting better. I started teaching her math again, and now she was paying attention. I asked why the bat mitzvah tape had made her cry.

"When I heard the Torah blessings," Ellen said. "I suddenly realized that not only was I going to fail in school but I would be missing my bat mitzvah too. I had worked a long time for that. I didn't really want to throw it away. But I was so weak. I didn't know if I could do it. That's when I started to cry."

Ellen reached over and hugged me.

"I don't know what I would have done without you, Lys. I kept trying to slip away, and you wouldn't let me. You kept coming back. You wouldn't let me go."

On Wednesday, Nadine announced that the second half of class would be used for working on individual problems related to *The Nutcracker.* I noticed that Jason and two other boys who sometimes come in for partnering were taking class with us.

"Those in lead roles requiring partnering will be working with Jason, Craig, and Paul," said Nadine. "The rest of you know where your weaknesses lie. If you need to strengthen your pointe work, now is the time to concentrate on those exercises. If it is flexibility, stretch. You all need to work on your bourrées."

"But, Nadine, how can we all play our music at the same time?" asked Amy Sue.

"Play your music in your heads, if you need it. Tomorrow we will work again as a class, and we will start putting it all together on the weekend."

There was no reason for me to remain. I might have worked at the barre, but having no part to practice for made it seem silly. At the end of the first half, I gathered my things and left.

I was a block away from the synagogue before I realized where I was headed. I walked in on the confirmation class's planning session for the annual youth service the following week. Members of the class would conduct the service themselves.

"Must we do it the way you do it, Rabbi?" someone asked, "or can we change it around a little?"

"There are certain prayers that must be said and a general sequence must be followed, but otherwise you have a free hand," said Rabbi Pearlman.

"Would it be okay to read my own poem instead of a psalm?" asked Mindy. She had been in Hebrew school with me. I hadn't known she wrote poetry.

"Sure," said the rabbi. "Words in praise of God have the same effect no matter what the source."

"Would the cantor mind if we sang some of the songs? Some of us are in the choir at school."

"This is your service. Cantor Weiss won't even be there unless you want him to be."

There was a general buzz of excitement in the room. They were lining up readers and singers. A burst of laughter escaped as they tried to decide who would best imitate Rabbi Pearlman. Everyone and no one wanted to do it.

I don't know why, but I raised my hand and asked if I could dance.

"Well, that's interesting, Alyssa, because dance

used to be part of the religious expression during other periods in history, although it is not common practice today. But won't your dance classes keep you too busy to work up something in so short a time?"

"Not anymore," I said. "I won't be in *The Nutcracker* this year, so I'll have plenty of free time."

Rabbi Pearlman raised his eyebrows in question.

I forced a smile from my lips.

"Ellen is doing better, Rabbi," I said.

He nodded.

"You'll work out the details with the rest of the confirmation class, Alyssa. This should be one very interesting service. I wouldn't miss it for the world."

The rest of the confirmation class—how easily Rabbi Pearlman absorbed me into it. The others didn't seem to mind. In fact, they crowded around me to ask about how long I had been dancing and where I took lessons. I began to feel part of the group. By the time I left, I had caught everyone's enthusiasm. I was actually excited about dancing in the youth service.

For the rest of the week, I divided my spare time between working on my research paper and trying to work up a dance for the service. I took out records from the synagogue library and brought them to Ellen's house. She still wasn't very strong, but we were able to do some schoolwork, and she started practicing her Torah and haftorah portions.

When she got tired, she listened to the records with me and helped me pick out a song to dance to. I discovered how lovely the service music is. I had always liked to listen to it in synagogue, but I thought it was only because Cantor Weiss sang so beautifully. Now I heard the melodies for themselves. Sometimes they made me cry.

I chose *"L'chah Dodi,"* the song that welcomes the Sabbath. Ellen watched me dance. When I tried new steps, she told me if they looked good or if they were wrong for the music. I noticed, at times, that she was humming along with the record. The ginger ale was coming back into her voice.

As Ellen got stronger, I started going to her house after dancing class as well as before. I still ached to be in *The Nutcracker*, but dancing to the Jewish music helped. It gave me something to do with my body, which was crying out to dance.

The more I listened to the music, the more it spoke to me. I used what Nadine had taught me, but it was more than the steps and the arms and the line I was dancing—it was the spirit. I felt the music. It swirled inside me, and I had to dance it out.

16 CHAPTER

The synagogue was filling up. Ellen sat right up front. She was much better now although still too thin. I promised to make her that ice cream sundae. She had to take it easy, and the doctor said she wouldn't be able to play sports for a few weeks, but she was going back to school on Monday.

The members of the confirmation class, including me, were sitting in the first row. My parents were there. So were Mr. and Mrs. Ruben. Mom had invited Aunt Carol. She waved at me. I returned a tiny, little wave but tried not to encourage her too much. I prayed she wouldn't boom out "Mazel tov!" at the end of the service. After all, it wasn't my service the way the bat mitzvah had been—it was a group effort. Could only six weeks have passed since then? So much had happened, it seemed like a lifetime.

Rabbi Pearlman introduced the confirmation class to the congregation and then stepped from the *bimah*. I saw Brad in the back with a couple of his friends. They had been part of the youth service last year. Brad said it did something to you when you took the rabbi's place. He was right. The familiar service suddenly was all new. The words were the same, but hearing them spoken by people my age made them more personal. How different the Sabbath candles looked after Mindy had lit them.

When the service ended, Brian invited everyone into the social hall for a special celebration of the Sabbath through dance. Everyone piled into the room and waited. I stepped to the middle of the floor. I was wearing a white leotard, white tights, and a white flared skirt. I felt like the Sabbath bride.

The words of my song echoed in my head: *L'chah*

133

dodi lik'rat kallah p'nay Shabbat n'kab'lah . . . "Come my beloved and greet the Sabbath bride." Cantor Weiss had agreed to sing while I danced.

The people-filled room disappeared. I was only aware of the cantor's beautiful voice and my movement. My whole body sang the song. It may not have been *The Nutcracker,* but I had a solo.

When I finished, there was a loud chorus of "Shabbat shalom" from the confirmation class. We shook hands and smiled as people came up to tell us how much they enjoyed the service.

"Shabbat shalom," I greeted everyone.

"Shabbat shalom," came the greetings in return.

"Great service," said Brad when he finally reached me. "I might even go as far as to say it topped last year's—but only by a little," he added.

"Good Sabbath, Alyssa," said a familiar voice behind me.

I turned around and stared at the person whose voice I would know anywhere. It was Nadine Perrin.

"Nadine!" I said, my mouth dropping open.

Nadine smiled. "I knew you were progressing, but I didn't realize how wonderful your dancing could be," she said. "You know, when a dancer has good technique but no feeling, we say she doesn't dance. Tonight you danced, Alyssa."

I swallowed back the lump in my throat.

"I didn't know you would be here, Nadine."

"Rabbi Pearlman called and asked me to come. We had a long talk before the service. He told me what you had done for your sick friend."

I just stood there, not knowing what to say.

"Maureen is having a little trouble getting the Soldier Doll part right. She asked if someone else could do it. I think you can catch up on the steps if you would like to come back to *The Nutcracker*."

Would I? I thought about those three missed rehearsals.

Nadine put her hand on my shoulder. "Even a statue's heart can melt once in a while," she said.

Aunt Carol burst through the crowd with a hearty "Mazel tov!" She grabbed me and turned toward Nadine.

"Isn't my niece a wonderful dancer?" she asked, beaming.

"Aunt Carol!" I said.

"Yes, yes, she is," Nadine said and smiled.

I couldn't believe it! Nadine said I was a wonderful dancer. So what if Aunt Carol had prompted her—Nadine never said anything she didn't mean. It's funny that I thought Judaism would take me away from my dancing. I found out it helped get me more into it. And I discovered that dancing could make me feel more Jewish. Mom was right; people are complicated.

"Aunt Carol, why don't you take Nadine to get some tea and cake? I have to find someone."

I found Rabbi Pearlman near the sweets table.

"Rabbi . . ."

"Ah, Alyssa, have a cookie."

I shook my head. I had something important to say.

"I spoke with Nadine," I said. "I'm back in *The Nutcracker*. Thank you."

Rabbi Pearlman grinned. "It wasn't my doing. I just made her aware of the kind of person you are, the kind of *Jewish* person. Seems to me, no one should be punished for doing mitzvot, and you've done a number of them recently, Alyssa."

"I'm going to be pretty busy again, Rabbi," I said, "but I thought maybe, after *The Nutcracker*, I might be able to come to confirmation class when I have time—if it isn't too late."

"It's never too late. But to be truthful, I always considered you part of it anyway," he said.

Rabbi Pearlman sure didn't give up easily. Without thinking, I leaned forward and kissed his cheek. Then I pulled away, embarrassed. I was really surprised when the rabbi, instead of being shocked, kissed me back.

"Shabbat shalom, Alyssa," he said.

Then I remembered I had something to give him.

"Don't go away, Rabbi," I said.

I dashed for the coatroom. I found my jacket and fumbled in the pocket for the paper bag I had slipped in just before leaving home. I rushed back. Rabbi Pearlman was talking with Mr. and Mrs. Ruben. I put the bag into his hand.

"Shabbat shalom, Rabbi," I said, and walked away.

I knew when Rabbi Pearlman had opened the bag and discovered Jarred Judaism. His laughter rang out in the Sabbath evening.